S.G. PUBLISHING

I0665355

RED RUBI
URBAN ROYALTY 2

A BOOG DENIRO **PRODUCTION**

S.G. PUBLISHING

RED RUBI is a work of fiction. Any resemblances to a person or locale is merely coincidental, and a product of the author's imagination.

If you purchase this book with a dull or missing cover, you have probably purchased an unauthorized or stolen copy. Therefore, S.G. Publishing will not be responsible for the content within.

S.G. Publishing
Bronx, New York
Email: sgpublishingllc@gmail.com
WEBSITE: BOOGDENIRO.COM

ISBN 13 – 978-0-9828144-7-5

First Trade Paperback Edition Printing
10 9 8 7 6 5 4 3 2 1
Printed in the United States

S.G. PUBLISHING

RED RUBI
URBAN ROYALTY 2

A BOOG DENIRO PRODUCTION

Previously in **Urban Royalty...**

The driver's side door of the Hellcat popped open. After an intense gaze, Rubi got into the passenger side and saw smoke coming from Charlie's curled lips.

"Baby girl," he said, smiling.

"Hey, Charlie..."

"My cutie," he replied, checking out this fresh piece of ass. While in the joint, he used to dream about moments like this one. Just looking at Rubi was making his manhood stretch out the front of his jeans. He was well endowed too. So Rubi noticed.

"That don't smell like weed," Rubi noticed and said.

"They call this *toochie*."

"Never heard of it," Rubi said, smacking her lips and eyeing Charlie's fine and fly ass.

"Wanna see what's hitting for?"

"My brother told me...*don't smoke nothing I didn't roll, or didn't see get rolled.*"

The synthetic weed was beginning to take its effect on Charlie. He was feeling it. *And feeling Rubi.* He turned the music on, and Jeremih sang:

...If it look this good ....I wonder how it taste...
...Baby if I touch yo body ...hear you scream my name...

THE 5 SENSES, that's what he had booming from the speakers as he sang along. And Rubi giggled because she thought it was *so* cute.

Charlie sat his Backwood down in the ashtray, then reached over Rubi's right shoulder and began unzipping

1

her jumper.

Rubi looked at him like he was crazy, and said, "What are you doing?"

"*I ain't no kid, Rubi...*" he told her while staring her dead in her eyes. He was also pulling the top portion of her umper down over her shoulders. "*This comes off.*"

"Charlie," Rubi said, covering her luscious brown sugar nipples with her hands. "There's people out here."

He grabbed her thick thighs, pulling them towards him. He yanked down her silk jumper even more. And to balance herself, Rubi released her juicy jiggling tits. He pulled the jumper down to her ankles, and seen her flesh colored G-string.

"I can't believe this...*Charlie...*"

He had her hemmed up with her limbs up. He licked his lips like a wildcat, grabbed hold of the elastic on her G-string and snatched it down over her hips and knees in one swift motion. "*Charlie...!*"

His head dipped low and she felt his tongue between the first two toes on her left foot. She felt kisses on her ankles and shins. She could feel his lips traveling up her thighs, then at her inner thighs closest to her vagina.

She had totally forgot the advance was unwanted, and reminded herself that she liked this man so much that he was the first thing on her mind when she woke up.

His mouth made its way to those brown sugar nipples and he sucked them feverishly. His hungry mouth didn't leave one portion of her juicy tits un-licked.

Inevitably, he ate her pussy, thumbed her asshole, and Rub experienced her first orgasm.

2

INTRODUCTION

SUMMER 2016

Well, well, well, as expected—my mother is still tripping. Not disappointed, or shocked, but super upset. She told my dad, Bish King, her version of what she suspected had gone down in the Hellcat with Charlie a couple weeks back, and right before that shootout.

Charlie is my dude now. But at that particular moment, we were just getting acquainted. And, he was actually giving me *face*, not *busting it open* in the Hellcat. Contrary to what my momma may think about me, I do have class and would never play myself or the family by fucking in a car, on a busy city street. See, what had happened was, Charlie had overwhelmed me. His touch, his tongue, it all came at once. I tried to stop him, I swear to god, but he took what he wanted. And that was a taste of me. *Rubi King. A bad red bone bitch.*

Like I was saying though, I am very classy. And you know what??? I don't give a fuck what Angel Ross-King may think. Let her tell it, the crotch of my body hugging greenish floral silk jumper by **Dir'Me**, being

3

wet was worse than the singer Avery Trap's white baby Tee being soaked with blood, due to two gunshot wounds unintended for her.

That tells moms would not hesitate to go right ahead and try to cut me out the will. She's pregnant too, expecting her third child. I did want a younger sibling. But that was ten years ago. So, I gotta start planning for my future now.

You may think I'm overreacting. Well, I'm not!

My brother Mes'siyah, y'all know exactly who he is, *thinks he's god because he was named after Christ*, slapped me. And my mother just sat there like she was a spectator and watched. Even told my daddy, who was also present that Sunday morning, to "*let it play out*". I'm supposed to be daddy's little girl. But I guess because Mes'siyah has taken over the illegal side of the family business, and he happens to be doing a good job, that makes ⁊ it open season on *Rubi*. Or, maybe it's because he's fucking that Daenarys Targaryen looking chick. *Looking like the dragon queen from* **Game of Thrones**. And she just so happens to be the District Attorney's daughter. I hope she burns his ass! Brother or not, he ever put his hands on me again, *hmmmph*, you'll see! He thinks he's the heir to the throne, but when it's said and done, I'll be wearing the crown.

Right now though, I have to figure out a way to get Avery Trap to sign with me and my new management company. I'll be nineteen in a couple days, and ever since she got shot, her streams on iTunes have quadrupled. *Wouldn't that be a dope birthday gift???*

4

To snatch her right from under my parents. I'm not cut out to be handling the illegal side of the family business, like my brother, but with this body of mine, these looks, my smarts, and the prestige that comes with the family name, I won't have any problems doing my numbers on the music side of things. I've already got a half million followers on Instagram, whom all respect my influence. So, yeah!

Hell, I even got Charlie's fine ass telling me my shit don't stink. Could use him for a little muscle, if I just so happened to need it. There's still a little bit of mystery to Charlie. Things I'd rather find out on my own, instead of googling his coochie-eating ass. Besides, at this point, he's still my lil secret. No one knows about us. Not even my BFF, Imani.

But you know men. They're so competent at fucking things up. But, they better watch out. It's me bitches! *Rubi motherfucking King! Game the fuck on!*

CHAPTER ONE

The asphalt and the concrete on 57th Street was still dampened from the rainfall. And anyone with effective nostrils could smell the scent of more downpour to come lingering in the air.

On that very street, less than a week ago, rising songstress Avery Trap had been shot twice in a barrage of gunfire while some top Philadelphia officials were less than a city block away. The block party had produced a huge turnout, and was organized by self-made millionaire and philanthropist Bish King's progeny, Mes'siyah. Also in attendance with the KING ENTERPRISES cofounder was his pregnant wife, *and business partner*, Angel Ross-King.

This shooting was a top priority for the Philadelphia police department. The mayor had been in attendance. State Senator Shafiq Rhoades had even dropped in with Congresswoman Mia Ortega. Because it was the 4th of July, and an event sponsored by the Kings, who happened to be big campaign donors. And the festivities became the backdrop for gun violence.

Bish was still reeling about the whole ordeal, as he was dead smack in the middle of it. Not only was Avery Trap signed to his music group, but he was with her that night. They were in photos with the politicians. Now his son was being asked to come in for questioning.

"*What the fuck was I thinking?*" Bish asked himself countless times while pacing back and forth and peering out at the Brooklyn Bridge from his New York City loft.

Just moment before he began walking in small circles, scratching his forehead and salt-and-pepper beard, he had received a phone call from his attorney with the Chief of police on the other line. The chief said, "We're putting two of our top detectives on this one, Mr. King. It would help if your son Mes'siyah would make arrangements to come in…" A lump had formed in Bish's throat.

Mes'siyah could go in and mislead them, or he could plead the fifth, thought Bish. *But he can't not go in.*

Bish also knew his son had spiraled out of control since he had given him the reigns. He had become someone other than the boy Bish had fallen in love with from the first time he held him in his arms. Bish knew Mes'siyah could and would contest the move, even if lawyers were to accompany him to the interview. *Staying away from the police is at the top of his list of things to do,* Bish reasoned. *And they should be. But…*

Thaila!, Bish thought while opening a brisk 16 ounce bottle of water and guzzling some.

Thaila was Bish's real estate agent. He slipped his android phone from the right back pocket of his PRP jeans. In two rings Thaila was on the line.

"Any word on that place out in Calabasas I asked you to secure for me and my wife?" Bish asked.

"Mr. King, two-point-five is what you have me working with. And I am working. But, nothing yet, sir. *Mmmmh.*"

"Are you okay?"

"Yes. Just, ah, fine."

"You're breathing seems a bit labored," Bish said, before taking another sip of the frosty beverage.

At that very moment, Thaila had company. And she *was* breathing a bit heavy. Mes'siyah had come to her office with lunch, and had just been feeding her his manhood. Mes'siyah was actually standing right in front of her, jeans and drawers down around his ankles, with his stick still erect and waiting for her lovely mouth to finish sucking him. With Bish on speaker phone, Mes;siyah could hear the worry in his father's voice, didn't like it one bit. So he directed his meat back towards Thaila's lips with a smirk on his face.

While kissing and licking the tip and the shaft, Thaila told Bish, "I will be ramping up the search...using...all my...resources...and; I mean, connections...on the west coast to get this...done. Is everything okay, sir?"

"Are you sure, you're okay is the question?" He was truly concerned. Thaila had helped secure the King compound, the loft in New York, the Pocono Mountain villa. She was instrumental in the securing of all their personal properties, as well as most of the stuff they'd been paid to restore, or bought and flipped, over the past few years

Mes'siyah pushed his dick deep into her mouth, while wrapping his ponytail around his fist. She could not talk. But Thaila was most certainly smiling and enjoying her young and secret lover's hypersexual behavior. Behind Bish's back, she had been fucking Mes'siyah. Initially she had wanted Bish. They were both married, and could carry on an affair, while still sharing their lives with their spouse, Thaila had proposed. But Bish declined. Although they weren't still madly in love, Bish was still loyal to Angel. So, Thaila entertained the next best thing. The younger and more energetic version of Biship King.

"Call me back when you have something," Bish said, then ended the call. *Real bosses never make their employees uncomfortable, if it isn't necessary.*

While Bish was trying to put as much space as possible between him and that shooting, his son was questioning whether or not he could continue to operate under his father's guidance. He knew his father had left the city with *opps* still running around, and Mes'siyah didn't respect that one bit. The family was attacked. And there were a lot of people who saw that as a vulnerability. And Mes'siyah refused to lose the stronghold that was just taking on its form under the *new King order* he was putting in place.

Cowardice was one thing, and cautiousness was another. But, Mes'siyah didn't know the difference between the two positions. He lacked sense sometimes, and had very little pragmatism. But he was still young, and had time to grow. *Or did he?*

On the other hand, Bish was of the school of thought that taught *intelligence over emotions*. He hadn't shot his recording artist, but he knew exactly who had. He saw the distinct and handsome features nestled beneath that head full of prosthetic dreadlocks. And he knew Smally G was no longer a threat, but a clear and present danger to Bish, and everything he loved.

CHAPTER TWO

"The Bronx. 175th Street, and Macombs Road," Bish told the driver upon entering the backseat of the big black 2016 Mercedes Maybach. It was about a thirty minute trek from where he had spent the last couple nights.

When he got to the Bronx, Mally Gz was standing out front of the five story tenement building he lived in, waiting. There were several building resembling that one lining both sides of the street, all connecting.

A small crowd of grown men, rather quiet, were occupying the stairs leading to the building's entrance. All five of these dudes gave Mally Gz dap and a thug hug as he left the fort.

As soon as he got in the back of the 'Bach, Bish said, "You still here?"

Mally Gz could see the evident disapproval of his uncle, by marriage. But he still said, "That's a fact."

"All that mutherfucking money you making, Jamal???"

"I gotta be here," Mally Gz said, taking off his aviator shades and New York Yankees snapback baseball cap.

"Why do you feel like you can't leave? Can't leave your boys behind? I never understood that. Ain't that what we hustle for? Take the chances we take? Make

11

The sacrifices we make? To get out of these densely populated traps? God forbid a pandemic hits, with black and Latinos all living right on top of each other," Bish sounded off, looking out the tinted window.

"You sound like you in a bad mood, Unc. I heard about the shooting on Independence Day. I was supposed to come through there. But wifey started having what we thought were contractions."

Their hands met, grasped tightly, then Bish said, "The internet is buzzing about it, because—"

"—Avery Trap was there, and sustained two slugs to that banging ass body," Mally Gz said, finishing Bish's thoughts. "She still breathing though. That's good."

"Your aunt was there too," Bish said, releasing the strong grip on Mally Gz's hand. "And your cousins."

"You looking stressed. The beard ain't died up and all that, grays poking out. What's popping?"

"I was there too."

"I be knowing, Unc. I be knowing. Wifey showed me some flicks of all y'all with the mayor and whatnot. Floating on the internet and shit."

A quietness fell upon them as the luxurious car drew attention. "Silvia's! Harlem," Bish ordered.

While they were picking at their food, neither man really had an appetite, Bish gave Mally Gz the game on what transpired and what he could have done different if he was thinking. What he didn't tell his nephew was, that prior to that shooting, he and Whispers had murdered Smally G's mother, a casualty of war. *That's what really bothered him.* But he could not reverse the hands of time. He had to be a forward thinker.

Mally Gz said, "Ever heard of Broward County?"

"A hop, skip, and jump from Dade County."

"What's up?"

This wasn't a laughing matter, but Mally Gz chuckled a bit, clapping his hands, then said, "Some of the best football players come out of Broward County. It's like a breeding grounds for elite wide-outs, monster running backs, and this new crop of mobile quarterbacks in the NFL."

"I do music, clothing, property restoration, own five car lots, but I don't do sports, Jamal. I watch 'em. But I don't do sports."

"Nah, see, Unc. My neighborhood is the same way for criminals. The *10453* is a breeding grounds for some of the most dangerous men in this city."

Bish just looked at him, thinking, *What the hell are you talking about???*, then chomped down on a thick barbeque chicken leg.

"If I leave, I won't know what's going on in these streets. I gotta have my boots on the ground with the troops. Gotta stay in the trenches, until I am totally out the life," Mally Gz explained. "Those are the terms I will be leaving on."

Mally Gz had two apartments side by side, with the conjoining wall knocked out, making his home in the hood a bit more hospitable. All five rooms were furnished immaculately, and every room had state of the art appliances, even the two bathrooms. And his rent was only two bands a month. And 'til he hit that seven figure mark, which he wasn't far from now, that's where he would reside. And when he did leave, the pad would be handed down to the next *block boss* up.

Bish said, "My kids don't know what it's like to struggle. To sacrifice. To deliberate where their next meal is gonna come from. Not like me. Not like your aunt Angel. *Not like you, Jamal.*"

"I think that's because they had a father in their lives. That is so important in cultivating culture today, Unc," replied Mally Gz, thinking of the absentee father he shared DNA with, and the eventual birth of the prince his queen was carrying.

Bish said, "Sometimes, I wish you were my son."

Mally Gz was at a loss for words. For one, Bish was larger than life, and just being able to eat with him was enough. But he was family. So the revelation came as a surprise, almost in the same way inspiration came to prophets when the Lord of all the worlds spoke to them.

Even at 25-years of age, full grown, stone to the bone, Mally Gz sensed a soft spot. He had always wanted to be a *King*. And if Bish asked to adopt him, he would not hesitate to say "yes".

See, Mally Gz didn't know who his father was. For years he believed some dude named Savage was his dad. Then when he was like nine, that sad day happened. On *Maury*, he watched Savage be told, "*You are not the father!*" And this savage ran around the stage shouting, "*See, I told y'all!*"

Mally Gz's heart was hardened from that day on. But those deliberate words that escaped Bish's thoughts had reversed the spell.

Sometimes, I wish you were my son...

Sometimes, I wish you were my son...

SOMETIMES, I WISH YOU WERE MY SON...!

Now Mally Gz was wondering what brought Bish to the city that never sleeps? To the point that they were having one-on-one meeting at a legendary soulfood joint in the newly gentrified Harlem? Made him also wonder about all that sadness in Bish's brown and serious eyes?

"Tell me something; what's the real story behind your aunt Angel and your grandmother Juanita's estrangement?" Bish inquired, while dabbing him lips and chin with a thick white napkin.

"She was diagnosed with bipolar disorder, post-traumatic stress disorder, antisocial personality disorder, and mild neurocognitive damage resulting from a traumatic head injury she suffered in a car accident back in 1977."

"The same year Angel was born?"

Mally Gz nodded. "It was a blackout that night, and word is, that's how the accident happened. Traveling in the darkness. Granny was going into labor, and they rushed her to Lincoln Hospital, in route, the car flipped over. They're both lucky to be alive. The driver didn't make it," Mally Gz explained just the way it had been given to him over the years.

"And, who was the driver?"

"My granddad, so they say."

Bish said, "Twenty-two years with Angel, and there's

still so much mystery to this woman. I'm here because
I need answers. And Angel won't tell me things I need
to know."

"Is everything cool?"

"We're expecting our third child, and I'm in the
process of moving her and the baby to the west coast.
And I just wanted to know if it would be a good idea to
bring your grandmother with us to help out. Now that I
know she has mental issues, I don't think it would be a
good idea."

"Another kid???" Mally Gz was surprised.

"Yeah, yeah. The queen gets what she wants. And
you, any day now, right," Bish said, trying to get the
waitresses attention. When she got to the table, Bish
gave her two c-notes and told her to keep the change.

Outside on the curbside sat the driver, ripped arms
folded across his brolic chest. The sun was beaming,
and so was his bald head. When he seen Bish emerge
with Mally Gz picking up the end, he opened the back
door so they could slide into the Maybach.

"So, tell me a little about your team. Those boys
holding down your fort..."

"If you want the best out of person, you go to the best
in that person. I've molded them in the image of me.
We don't hustle we don't eat, we don't grind, we don't
shine. If need be, we gonna let the guns go. But we
stack paper before we resort to violence. And we
always make sure you and Auntie Angel are straight
first."

Those type of conversations went on for the next two

days. *Meetings of the minds*, as Bish often would call them.

Bish was planning for the future. And there was just no way the future of the brand he sacrificed his life building would be solely vested in Mes'siyah. His son was too much of a hot head. And, no question treachery had its place in the game. But, it wasn't a recipe to continued success. And with Smally G on the prowl, and a bloody onslaught in the makings, preparations for the future were mandatory in Bish's book.

CHAPTER THREE

Back in Philly...

"So, Mr. Smallwoood, this is your second appoint-ment since your release from state prison."

"Yes, that is a fact," Smally G said to his parole officer, a woman he was looking at with sad eyes.

"And, I understand you're requesting permission to attend your mother's funeral in Charleston, South Carolina? Is that correct?"

"Correct," Smally G replied, while also nodding.

"I am sorry for your lose."

Smally G just nodded again, eyes glazed a little.

"Okay, I have to run this by my supervisor since you are a convicted murderer. I'll give you a call."

"Thank you," Smally G said, then dipped. When he got out to the curbside, he checked his missed calls and messages. A video of Mes'siyah came up in his timeline on Instagram. He was beginning to really hate Mes'siyah as much as he hated Angel and Bish.

Mes'siyah was livestreaming himself in New York's Diamond District. Mally Gz was close by, but not in the camera. MES'SIYAH in solid gold with white ice all through it swung from a super thick gold Cuban link.

"My masterpiece is finally complete! Thirty bandz on a chain and piece! Twenty-four carats set in twenty-four karat gold. *Ice cold!*"

Smally G wasn't the only hater watching Mes'siyah. The Trap God and his man, the one Mes'siyah shot, was watching the video as well. Mes'siyah had almost a half of a million followers, and he was following about one thousand users, mostly celebs.

It was also Rubi King's nineteenth birthday. So Mes'siyah copped her a piece of jewelry too. It may seem unbelievable, but he actually used to sing his sister's praises. She as a straight-A student, so he would brag about her all the time. "*My sister is smart, she ain't no thot! And she ain't fourteen with a baby!*" he used to say. But he was also a different person back then as well. The two siblings had the same joys, were super tight, and inseparable. So no one was struck with surprise when he shouted her out on his platform on her birthday.

"Shouts to my sis, Rubi King. Happy B-day! I got you something too." For the world to see, Mes'siyah opened a pretty black velvet box. The box had width and some length to it. He opened it, revealing a solid gold tiara with diamonds and rubies all through it. "I'll see you tonight at your party. *We gonna do it up*! Kings for life..."

Rubi was shocked, because they weren't on the best terms. She instantly LOVED it. It just so happened to be one of Mes'siyah's most viewed videos ever.

"What you looking at?" Smally G asked Rubi, as he

took a seat in the rented Range Rover he had her driving. He still had his phone in his hand, watching the Instagram Live. There was a lot of bass in his voice, and Rubi immediately peeped it. It was her birthday and she wanted to enjoy it.

"Oh, nothing," Rubi said, gazing at Smally G.

"You obviously looking at something," Smally G said, fondling Rubi's left breast while putting his nose to her neck and inhaling her lovely scent.

"I'm looking at you," she said, real sassy. "Kiss me," she then ordered Smally G.

Though Smally G was mourning his mother, and the details surrounding her murder was sketchy, he was still full of life. Still plotting his revenge against the Kings. Shooting Avery Trap was nothing compared to what he had planned for them.

The kiss was intense, as he fondled Rubi a bit more, cupping both of her tits now. Then he told her to pull off in the marine blue Range Rover.

As they traveled, Smally G finalized the funeral arrangements. Rubi drove out to the hotel they planned to stay in, the whole time enjoying Smally G's hands all over her. It was hot that day, so she wasn't wearing much: short shorts and a tank top, no panties, no bra. And Smally G was loving it. He had managed to slip his hand beyond the crotch of Rubi's shorts and Rubi grinned.

"It's my birthday!" she sang, whipping the Range.

"That indeed it is..." Smally didn't know it, but Rubi had yet to be deflowered. She had been real strict with her goodies. Not because she was saving herself for marriage, or scared of dick, but because she actually knew the power of pussy. And, Rubi wielded it with precision. But, tonight Smally G was going to be the first to bust it open.

At the next red light, Rubi reached down into Smally G's joggers and got hold of his manhood. With his dick in her hand, she was ready to rebel, ready to rejoice, ready to revolt. In an erotic move, the two kissed while pleasuring each other.

Horns began to blare and honk, because they were now holding up traffic. The light had turned green again.

"What does *Dir'Me* stand for?" asked Smally G, as he traced the cursive lettering on the front of her tank top with is right index finger.

Rubi began to drive again, and said, "It's an acronym, Charlie. And, it means: *Don't Ignore Responsibility; Manage Emotions...*"

Everything the brand stood for, Rubi King was now going against.

Not only was her shirt baring the designer's name, but so was her cute little pink shorts. Rubi had bright hazel eyes and bowlegs. She was 5-foot-2 with a tiny waist, shapely hips, athletic thighs and a pretty butt. She also had marvelous c-cup breasts that seemed to bring eyes to the red-bone everywhere she went. The girl was gorgeous. No one could deny that. And all that beauty had Smally rethinking his master plan.

See, it had always been in his mind that he would tear

the King family apart from the inside out.

From the moment he found out Bish had been released from prison, charges dismissed, while he was going upstate with a twenty year bid, Smally G felt like the fix was in.

The summer of 1996, Bish had lured Smally G's robber back out to West Philly, then told Smally G exactly where he would be. When the stickup kid got to the scene, Bish told Smally G, "Market Street. Red Audi." Smally G walked up on the driver's side, and fired six rounds into the foreign car, then ran to the side street where Bish was waiting in an all black Honda Accord station wagon. At the time they were street partners, flipping a big eighth once a week. But by player standards, they were barely scratching the surface.

Just a day after the shooting, they were both apprehended on a street corner, and arrested for first degree murder. One became an inmate, amputated from the community, while the other outlaw prospered.

Bish took full advantage of his freedom, while Smally G filled his mind with vengeance. Had Bish gone on to thrive with any other woman by his side, besides Angel, Smally G would have congratulated and saluted the business mogul. But Bish had to have Angel. And in Smally G's eyes, Angel was his first. His property. He had gone to the Bronx, New York and discovered her. He saw the fly girl, with the mean flow, and hustle, from New York as his.

Back then, a lot of street cats who were into rap music

*thought Angel Ross was destined to roc the mic, on a big stage. She had rhymes for days, and she had the **it factor**. Smally G saw Angel and her talent as his way out of the streets. But Bish saw more. He saw his future Queen.*

Bish's ability to image was his most powerful tool. He also saw imagination as its own form of courage. And it wasn't like he waited to Smally G took his fall from the game to scoop her, Bish was on her top while Smally G was still a free man and acting a fool. And, at the end of the day, it was Angel's decision whether she wanted to be *Smally G's rap artist*, or *Bishop King's muse*.

And surely Angel had inspired Bish.

$ $ $

Upstairs in the hotel suite, Rubi dropped her bags, center floor, while Smally G took to the bathroom. He shut the door behind him. And there he wept, mourning the woman who had brought him into this cold world. He lived by that foolish code – *never let 'em see you cry*. But that day, the dams, better known as his eyes, had broken. His face was wet with tears. He hadn't even cried when he was sentenced to two decades. But this one hurt. Because, he knew she was dead because of him. His brother Mar didn't have many enemies, and definitely none bad enough to take their mother out. This had *Whispers* written all over it, piano wire to the neck, and Smally G knew it. But old Whispers wouldn't make a move like that, unless Bish ordered it.

His brother Mar had been blowing his phone up with texts about who he thought could be responsible, and that just infuriated Smally G.

He shut his phone off.

And then he began to wonder if he was even as cold and callous as he had portrayed for so many years while in prison. Death did things like that to people. Made them question everything. He didn't even want to shoot the dude in the red Audi back in 1996, the dude who'd robbed and stripped him in the middle of the streets. *But, he didn't want to disappoint Bishop King.*

Smally G was so caught up in his thoughts, he didn't even hear Rubi slip into the bathroom. With troubled eyes, he just looked up as she sat in his lap where he was perched on the side of the huge white porcelain bathtub.

"Rubi said, "I've never seen a man cry…"

Smally G really broke down, weeping uncontrollably.

He had spent 20-plus years in prison, and not once did his mother visit him. He would write her letters, send cards, get portraits made, and she would never reply. Every year around Christmas, a card would come under his door, addressed from her, *but signed in his brother Mar's name.*

But when she heard Smally G had made parole, she sent him the new address, and a car to pick him up. When he got to her new home, that he wondered how she could afford on her budget, there was a huge feast on the table. The two had eaten mostly in silence. Fish, ribs, chicken, all kinds of salads and sides. Then over some fresh bread pudding smiles emerged. His mom told him she wanted more for him when he was growing up, and that he needed to take back what Bishop King had taken from him. She told Smally G, Bish had been setting her out with loot for bills over the years, but that he still owed their family. And that he had even purchased her a home. But that wasn't enough reparation. Ended by telling Smally G, he better never let the cops put cuffs on him again. *Now she was gone. Crossed over to the next life.* And the head of her 42-year-old son was buried in the bosom of his nemesis's 19-year-old daughter.

His phone began to buzz. He thought it was his younger brother, Mar, again. But it wasn't.

"Rubi, let me take this. I'll be done in a minute."

Rubi kissed the left corner of his mouth, then departed, leaving the door slightly ajar.

Immediately, Smally G took the call, and the woman on the other end said, "Hello!!!"

"Yeah, what's good?"

"Excuse me?" the woman said, snidely.

"What's up?"

"*Humph!*" she blew like an exhaust pipe.

Smally G exhaled then inhaled deeply. "Antonita, what up?"

"When the fuck is you coming to see my mother-fucking son? That's what's up!" spat the Puerto Rican mother of his three-year-old son. "You been home for a week and a half now, nigga, and you haven't checked in yet. On me, or your son."

"You know I just lost my mother."

"Okay. But what about before that? You was supposed to stop here before you went anywhere. That's what we discussed didn't we?"

"That's a fact. But shit came up. And I want to give my undivided attention when I come through."

"Yeah, okay. Don't forget I pulled a lot of strings for you. I made a lot of sacrifices. I ain't just no baby mother. I got a badge, and a gun, nigga."

The bathroom in the hotel suite was so big, and the tub was situated in the back, Rubi couldn't really hear much. But she did hear Smally G say, "*I always take care of mines. If I'm rocking with you, it's till the wheels fall off...*"

When Rubi heard the soles of his Balenciaga sneakers squeaking against the tiled bathroom floors, she slipped back onto the oval bed and propped herself up on her elbows where she lay looking in Smally G's direction. One foot was planted at the edge of the bed, while the other just dangled.

"I gotta make a quick run," he said, scooping the car keys up off the table.

Rubi sucked her teeth as the room door slammed shut behind him.

CHAPTER FOUR

Five-foot-eight for a woman is kind of tall. Not runway tall, but just as tall as the average American male. Avery Trap had the looks to go with the height. She resembled a brown skinned Christina Aguilera.

"I see you finally made it out to see me, Mr. King."

"Of course, Avery. Would have been here sooner, but I had business in New York."

"My hometown," Avery Trap said, while elevating her hospital bed so that she could see Bish better. She went on to say, "I came to *Illadel* to perform at your son's event, because you asked me to. There were no contractual obligations whatsoever. And now I'm going back to New York with gunshot wounds."

Normally Avery Trap would've been gushing at the sight of Bishop King. She found men in their forties to be very attractive. The salt-and-pepper hair and all. *Not too much salt though.* But especially men who painted portraits of gallantry with their actions. She knew Bish as a chivalrous man packed with charm. And loved the way he dressed, addressed, and effortlessly impressed. Not this day. Her executive producer would not be getting any gushy smiles. There was no amazement in Avery Trap's slanted eyes. And ...venom saturated her

27

sultry voice.

Bish couldn't help but notice and understand the vehement defiance in his artist's demeanor. And the disdain in her scowl. *Professionalism*, he told himself. *Human relations*, he inwardly added. As the thoughts invaded his mind, Avery Trap ascended from beneath the white bed sheets by Boll&Brand which had been dropped off by Rubi.

Avery Trap got close to Bish, and she said, "Those bullets weren't meant for me. Were they?"

"I can't answer that, because I'm not investigating the matter. Let's leave that for the cops to figure out."

Avery Trap said, "But, I saw you with a gun. Your son and his crew were packing. And you were all firing back. So, I'm thinking, someone has to know something. This was supposed to be a family function, and my performance was a charitable one."

Bish could smell the sexy songstress's breath, that's how close she was to him. He looked back over his shoulder. The door was still secure, with an armed guard on the other side.

"Being able to control your attitude, regardless of your circumstances is the best characteristic one can have. Everything else is the byproduct of that attitude, Avery."

"You also told me – *success without fulfillment is the ultimate failure*. And, that, *you miss one hundred percent of the balls you don't swing at*. And, that, *when people settle we deserve everything we get*."

"I did say those things. I said them to you because, I

live by them. Philosophy is so necessary in life."

Avery Trap's room was filled with balloons and flowers, from fans, family and friends. And, Rubi had dropped a lot off herself while pitching her proposal to become Avery Trap's new manager.

Avery added some water to the tulips and roses, then she pulled the blinds in her window a bit tighter so that no one could see inside.

"Two detectives came to see me."

"And what were they saying?"

"Well, the Columbo cat was talking like it was his destiny to bring my shooter to justice. But he also thinks you were the target of this shooting."

"He said that?" Bish boomed.

"In a roundabout way. I know he knows you're not just some music impresario. Or some trendy fashion designer. He had this feel of an old eighties era lawman."

"I know who he is."

"Maybe it's time you do what you've been telling me you're gonna do for the last six months."

"Leave my wife and family, and run off with you?"

"Exactly. I almost lost my life fucking with you, being loyal to you. No one knows about us, and that's because I kept my end of the deal."

"If people find out now that you're sleeping with the label head, while my wife is carrying our third child, your streams, which have risen since this unfortunate event, could very well plummet."

"You told me you were going to make me the next…"

"To come out the Bronx. I know what I said, and I upheld my end of the bargain. I put a quarter million behind you. Because, I believe in you."

"So, what about me becoming the next Mrs. Bishop King? What have you done to begin that process?"

Bish decided to look around the air conditioned hospital room instead of answering that. His hands touched the strings from the balloons that had floated to the ceiling. He reached for the bouquets of flowers. Even picked up one of the tiny cards that was on the dozen of long stemmed white roses.

The card read,

I'm here for you sis. You already know!
Love, Rubi King

"Oh, you two calling each other sisters now?" Bish quizzed, turning back around to face Avery Trap.

"Well, she made it clear when she came by that she's looking to be more than my play-play sister."

"And that means exactly what?"

Avery Trap ran her hand over Bish's right lapel, real seductive like. It wasn't something she hadn't done before. In fact, she'd done it numerous times. But this time her hand didn't stop there.

Bish pushed her hand away from his crotch area, held her left wrist rather firm. He then said, "Not until you tell me what you meant when you said my daughter is looking to become more than your play-play sister."

Avery Trap huffed and puffed, like women do when

30

They're about to express themselves in a forceful manner. She said, "You're daughter asked to manage me!! She came by last night with her dude. He looked familiar, like I'd seen him before. Now, can you relinquish my arm, Bishop King?"

"Her dude?"

"Yeah. I'm not the only one looking to be taken serious."

"Listen, when this started, you told me you prefer to be the mistress. Don't' you forget that."

"And when you found out I know how to rock more than just a mic, you made sure that I knew you weren't exactly happy in your marriage. Isn't that why you took me to Atlanta with you back in April? Told Angel you were meeting up with Tyler Perry about a potential film deal?"

"She was forcing me to have another child," escaped Bish's curled lips.

The truth of the matter was, Bish loved Angel dearly, but he wasn't in love with her anymore. She was no cupcake on the assembly line. In fact, she was a problem when she wanted to be.

Bish wanted to get out of the business, and she wanted to continue tossing bricks at the prisons. It had actually been her idea to put Mes'siyah in charge of things. She thought his youth and energy, along with his vicious crew, would bring the numbers back up to where they were when they were in their prime. Bish wanted to give the reigns to his main man Whispers, and ride off into the sunset. Just run his recording label, the clothing line, the car dealerships and the restoration company, *all remotely*. Of course, with staff in place. Just spend the next twenty or thrity years with is family, and not in a federal penitentiary because he didn't listen to his conscience.

Bish also knew that Smally G was up for parole, and pretty much wanted to be out of the way when Smally G pulled back up. This way, any tension over what he considered betrayal wouldn't have to be played out in the streets.

But when Mes'siyah had asked Bish was he trying to leave Philly for Calabasas, because he knew Smally G was on his way home, Bish had played it off like he'd been insulted and his pending release was news to him.

Bish was a smart man, extremely cerebral, but one would never know it by the way he'd been acting over the last couple months. He didn't acquire so much being emotional, it was through his elite street acquired intelligence that he rose high in the ranks. He had really been in the streets, taking money, manipulating scenarios, ducking police, breaking down bricks to the very last compound. And then, moneybag stashing along the way.

Along with Angel's finesse, they went corporate. Now, it was all on the verge of destruction. Becoming a colossal failure. *Unless he turned things around.*

Angel would never let him go, so divorce was out the question. She didn't have eyes for another man, so she wasn't about to separate. The only way out that marriage was through death.

"Avery, I'm gonna need some more time."

"That's the same thing I told your daughter."

"She has no management credentials, or skills, so I'm not worried about that. In fact, I don't even want her to know that you told me she tried to pull this stunt. You hear me, Avery?"

"Bish, Bish, Bish..."

"What?"

"Don't lighten up, tighten up, before it's too late," Avery Trap warned Bishop King, then gave him her back.

Bish reached out to touch her, then thought otherwise. He let himself out, shaking his head.

CHAPTER FIVE

Back at the hotel...

Upon Smally G's return, Rubi jumped in his face immediately. Like, wasted no time. "You left me here for *hours*! *What the fuck!*"

"Calm down, before I calm you down,"Smally G warned Rubi with a smile on his face that appeared to have a light coat of perspiration on it, making his deep brown skin look shiny. He then shook his head, walking pass Rubi towards the big oval shaped bed the two new acquaintances would be sharing if things ever heated up like she anticipated they would.

He couldn't help but think that while he was eating Rubi's pussy in the Hellcat a few days back, her father, and his crony *Whispers* were putting the old trusty piano wire to his mother's neck, depriving her of what little air her precious lungs could take at her old age.

Ice cold!

He could hear Bishop King saying as he watched her soul leave her body.

Smally G had no proof Bish was responsible, except that he had waged war against the Kings when he went up to New York and stormed their little shindig, pulling a weapon in the process.

With that, he blamed himself. Smally G knew he was slipping instead of stalking, while Bish was creeping and chalking.

"Excuse me, Charlie! And, that means exactly what? Calm me, *whaaaa*?" Rubi asked smoothly, gripping her shapely hips at the same time. Mes'siyah and Angel were the only two people who could get away with talking slick to her. And occasionally her bestie Imani. But there wasn't another soul walking, *or rolling*, God's green earth who could.

This man is rehabilitated. The level of direction, the ability to do things that are productive and inspiring and meaningful is profound. He is worthy of parole, he recalled the parole man saying at his hearing. *He has accepted responsibility, and accountability for what he had done*, the man had added.

Those words played in Smally G's mind as he took his shirt off and folded it neatly. He then said, "I'm sorry for leaving you in here alone, Rubi."

Rubi's eyes went to his toned body, the six pack in his stomach, the definition in his chest and shoulders, to the sight of his back muscles being visible even though she was looking at his torso. She could not deny Smally G was a man, and Trap God, *the dude she originally planned to give her virginity to*, was a boy. He had money like a man, but he was built like a boy. And, accepting responsibility was beneath the Trap God.

"I accept your apology," Rubi said, gushing with joy. The fact that she had planned to ask him where he had gone, and who he had been talking to that prompted the urgent escape didn't even cross her mind.

Smally G kicked his sneakers off, then unbuckled his YSL belt before slipping out of his jeans. He folded them neatly, sat them in a plush leather chair that was stationed in front of a huge smart TV anchored to the wall. That's where Rubi had been sitting in his absence.

Rubi now watched him in just his boxer-briefs and ankle socks marveling about the muscles in his calves and thighs.

Smally G wasn't saying much, too busy thinking. In just a couple weeks of being released from prison, he had shot someone, pulled a gun on Angel and Bish, stashed almost a half million in a safe deposit box he got off Bish, was about to bury his mother, whom he believed Bish killed or had killed, and now he was about to monster fuck Bish's daughter.

He didn't know she was a virgin. Hadn't been deflowered as of yet. He was certain she'd been passed around at a few gangster parties, or got mushy over some industry cat. Or, maybe even fucked her brother.

Smally G's mind was twisted. Had been even since he started smoking that *Atomic Bomb*, a synthetic cannabis, while behind the wall doing that 20 year bid. He started doing it to numb the pain, to escape his reality, then it became a nasty addiction that altered minds. He actually thought he functioned better under that influence. Boy was he wrong. *But there was no one to tell him.* He listened to no one. He only gave orders.

His alleged affiliation with Bish had given him immense power on the compound. Key word, *alleged*.

36

And *alleged* because, he had worn out any welcome with Bish early on in his bid. It hadn't been Bish who had discontinued their friendship, it had been Smally G writing the threatening letters. It had been Smally G getting hostile with Bish every time Bish had taken one of his calls. Bish switched his number on Smally G the winter of 1998, and warned that anyone caught giving Smally G the number would spend the rest of their life in a wheelchair. Bish said he wasn't going to kill the person, but most certainly paralyze him or her. And that was because Smally G had called Bish one cold night in December talking very aggressively. He had even told Bish that he was going to sodomize Angel and make Bish watch. When Bish began checking him, he tried to clean it up, by saying, *"She was mine first. But damn, nigga, lighten up. Bros over hoes!"*

At that time, Angel had just given birth to Rubi. As a matter of fact, Rubi had just taken her first steps. On top of that, Bish and Angel had just gotten married.

The two had spoken a few times after that, and Bish had even given Smally G twenty grand for a PCRA attorney to file a motion for a new trial even after the lawyer had told Bish the chances of Smally G giving back that guilty plea was slim to none. *Who was he to piss on a man's hopes and ambitions???* Plus, the money was flowing by then, and plentiful.

But the sand that blinded the camel was when Smally G had been telling people that Mes'siyah was his son. And, had even petitioned the courts for a paternity test.

As the story goes, Bish sent a dude up to the prison

to see Smally G with a personal message. Dude was supposed to slip a mickey in Smally G's soda bottle before he left the visit. But as fate would have it, Smally G didn't do vending machines on the visiting floor. He was took shook the police might think he was trying to sneak in some contraband and put him in a dry cell for three days. A dry cell consisted of being in a locked up alone, with nothing, draped in a flimsy hospital gown, ordered to give three solid shits that would be examined thoroughly before you were released from that hell. Oh, and the prisoner would be cuffed to the bed, twenty-four hours a day.

Smally G had dodged that bullet. But he also would dodge questions when asked about Bish. He allowed people to think that he and Bish were still tight, even fronting like he had just spoken to Bish when in fact he was really on the phone with someone else. Smally G was so vicious, he had taken some pictures from a magazine and sent them to a photo company so the photo company would send them back in the form of real photos. He then took them to the yard and said that Bish had just wrote him.

The letter that he had his young boys reading was saying some good shit. But, Bish didn't write him. The guy living next door to Smally G had written it and signed it *From Bishop King*.

And while Bish was on the outside blowing up, Smally G was on the inside living large too. Any drugs came through the compound, Smally G got his hand on it. Cellphones, Smally got to touch it.

Most of his connections came from the respect and fear and admiration dudes had for Bish. *He benefitted tremendously.*

The young boys he aligned himself with were gang-bangers, mostly filled up with unfounded and un-necessary wolf-pack syndrome rage, just hell-bent on self-destruction.

Smally G even bagged a couple C.O. bitches off his connections to Bish, and had one of them moving for him heavy.

The hand is truly faster than the eye. And Smally G was as slick as they come.

Smally G began to kiss Rubi passionately. Rubi was incredibly attractive from head to toe, and she had Smally G fawning all over her. He hadn't had anything as tender since he was a teenager making his bones on the street corners. While his tongue was all down her throat, he slipped out his boxer-briefs and was now wearing only his ankle socks.

Rubi felt him place her hand on his penis, and she took a step back. She couldn't believe she had his big dick in her small hand. It was hard, every fucking inch. And, pointing upward towards her chin. She licked her lips, bit down into the bottom one, then slowly shook her head in amazement. He didn't even have to do it. She was no longer concerned with being deemed immoral by her mother. She was no longer consumed with what Mes'siyah thought of her. Rubi did it herself.

"That's right, girl. That's right. Yeah...."

After she removed her top and shorts, Smally G began sucking her nipples intently. Both of them, back and forth, one at a time. His hands were full with her tits, and her hands were grasping his head.

"That feels so good, but I want you to eat my pussy, like you did in the Hellcat. No one has ever eaten my pussy like that, Charlie..."

Smally G tossed her little ass up on the bed. And she went flying. Giggled as her fat rump hit the sack. Smally G dove in, sliding right between her thighs.

Her pussy was bald with inner lips that didn't' exceed her fat outer ones. It didn't look beat up and abused, but preserved, delicate and delectable. Smally G could see her clit upholstered at the top of her slit. He went right for that with the quickness.

"*Ooooh...Charlie*" Rubi cooed, making Smally G grin and snicker feverishly.

He was grinning because no one called him Charlie. The name *Charlie* had died decades ago. Even his mother called him Smally. His real name was Charleston Smallwood. So, the Smally came from his last name. Charlie had been his sandbox name, which he carried till about the seventh grade.

Rubi was tasting good to him, and he was lapping at her vagina with passion. It was like he had all the time in the world too. The nigga turned on his side, between her legs, and ate her from that angle. When the panting picked up even more, he spun onto his back and made her sit on his face.

"*Charlie, this is the best birthday ever...*" she chimed

bucking rhythmically on his orifice.

Then abruptly he flipped her off of him, and pushed her down on the mattress. His hand was in the small of her back, and the other was on the nape of her neck. This was force she never knew. It was reminiscent to the scene in the Hellcat, on the side street when he ripped her panties from her flesh and dined on the wetness between her thighs. So she didn't know whether to be scared or excited.

"What are you doing?"

She felt the head of his penis up against her fleshy folds as her legs were slightly ajar from his moving them open with his knees. He used her juices to lubricate the tip of his member, then he caressed it against her anus.

Immediately she began to think about the bad press on brother imprisoned when it came to sexual desires. All the homosexual stuff. And she began to wonder. She also tried to turn around. But his manpower was just too much.

She looked so pretty under his power. Her bowlegs, her round ass, her back and shoulder blades. Everything about her said *beauty*. And he could not go through this is plan.

Suddenly, Rubi felt him release her. Like, absolutely removed his hands from her body. She looked over her shoulder first. Then rolled over onto her ass and just stared at him.

"Don't you have a party to be at tonight?" he asked.

"I do."

"Well make sure you get your ass back here, when it's said and done. Don't have daddy waiting."

"Okay. I'm with that."

"Then what?"

Rubi said, "What was that about, just now?"

He planned to make sure she couldn't walk for the rest of the night. He planned to give her a good reaming. He planned to punish her for her father's sins.

"What was that? What just happened?"

"I just told you. Now make sure you don't keep me waiting too long."

Rubi shrugged her shoulders, smiling, then looked at his dick, which was now becoming flaccid but still had some girth and length. She thought she was going to be attending her party with that pussy busted wide open. But, she would have to wait. Still, she touched it with her pointy fingernails, and said, "That's mine, right?"

Smally G, unable to give her his full attention, said, "Only if you put it in your mouth?

"When I get back, *I'll try*," she said with certainty and lust in her eyes. That made Smally G look. "Can I hit your blunt before I take a shower and leave to go get dressed?"

"Sure."

Rubi did not know that his blunt was laced with poison. She lit it up, and took two puffs and then another three. Long hard puffs too. Totally forgetting what her brother told her about not smoking shit she didn't roll. Within a split second the hotel suite flipped upside down, started spinning around, and she collapsed as her legs became wobbly, and she inevitably lost her footing on a well carpeted floor. Still conscious, but undoubtedly out of her mind, Rubi began talking in riddles.

Smally G raced to her side, and knelt like knight in shining amour, as Rubi muttered, "Clearly, or unclearly, nigga? Clearly or unclearly, you are not the true heir to the throne? Clearly or unclearly, nigga? Is it true that I may very well be my father's firstborn? Clearly or unclearly?" Her words held little context, seemed undeliberate, and were a mix of singsong at first to Smally G. He scooped her up into his arms as her eyes began to look glazed over and her lips began to curl up into a devilish grin.

His form of escape from reality was known to alter realities. He'd had his bouts with the subconscious mind playing tricks on him, from overdosing on it. He also knew that a person's inner thoughts could float to the front of their mind while in this state. Either from paranoia, or repressed thoughts.

Rubi continued to ramble. "I'll suck ya dick right now, Charlie. Pull it out. Put it in my mouth. I'll suck it now, if you let me suck it later."

Smally G's mind was somewhere else. *If Rubi could possibly be Bishop's true firstborn seed, then who is Mes'siyah's father?* He then looked into her eyes, and the more important words muttered resonated. *You are not the true heir to the throne.*

You are not the true heir to the throne.

You...are...not...the true heir...to...the...throne.

43

A sibling rivalry was brewing, that much Smally G knew for sure. And he hoped Rubi would do some more talking. More importantly, he could come to truly benefit if she were the true heir to the throne. And, if played his cards right, there could very well be a handsome reward at the end of this war. Did Rubi have dirt on her mother? Had Angel been cheating on Bish too? Did Bish know he might've raised another man's child? Or was Rubi just out of her mind?

CHAPTER SIX

Penelope was just ambling aimlessly around the ground floor of the King compound. She really didn't want to attend Rubi's 19th birthday party. But the entire staff were required to be in attendance. To show some structure and civility within the family. The King name had been being dragged through the tabloids, and Angel thought the pristine staff she herself assembled would look better there than lounging around her mansion.

After Avery Trap was shot, it brought bad publicity to the King brand. The streams were up, Avery Trap's music was playing more frequently on radio and satellite radio. The entire roster, which only consisted of five acts, were benefitting. But Young Sheemi and Avery Trap were buzzing.

So, in an attempt to remove the family name from up under the iron fist of bad press, Angel assumed responsibility as party planner.

Immediately, she found a new venue in Center City with a bigger ballroom. She then reached out to the press and a couple of local bloggers looking to get in her good graces, with the new location.

There would be no thugs standing on the wall, lighting up drugs. Strictly local socialites and squeaky clean kids from Temple and Drexel Universities. She had to control the narrative or risk losing everything.

Angel also reached out to the one boy she knew Rubi was fond of...

Trap God couldn't believe his eyes when a message from Angel Ross-King popped up in his DM.

Yeah, Angel had been monitoring his social media, and thought he had potential if he could stop putting all his business in the streets like work.

He is cute though, Angel said, rubbing her stomach, which was beginning to stick out a little. When he asked if his boys could tag along, she agreed to allow one. And no guns.

Just as Angel was about to reach out to her nephew Mally Gz, Penelope walked up with a duster in her hand.

"Girl, you know you ain't dusting nothing, so stop it," Angel said, and they both laughed. Penelope was a good housekeeper, but she was really around for her own personal reasons. She knew Angel knew that she was fucking Mes'siyah.

"Is there anything in particular that you would like the staff to wear to the party tonight?" she asked Angel.

"Formal would be appropriate."

"So work attire?"

"It would give off the vibe that you all left work to join the family. And you know how you like your little skirts, anyway. Mes'siyah will be there."

"Clearly, he will be there," Penelope said, gushing.

As soon as Penelope walked off, Angel sent an invite

to Ivory. *Might as well keep the Mannings in pocket too*, she said as she pressed send.

Penelope was very attractive and would probably make a good wife for Mes'siyah. But Ivory's father was the District Attorney of Philadelphia. *The daughter of the DA, or an immigrant from Brazil who snuck into the country with a caravan?*

Penelope had been with the Kings for seven years. She had raven hair that she kept in two long French braids pulled to the back with baby hairs laying down on her oatmeal colored forehead and temples. She was about to turn thirty, but was giving the young Instagram models hell.

Right after she left Angel on her Apple Mac computer, Penelope walked to the front of the mansion and peered out the window. *There was still a few hours before they were to arrive at the ballroom.* That's when she saw Rubi strolling through the gates, past the guards, and up to the side door that lead to the staircase closest to the side of the house where her room was.

"Are you okay, Rubi?" she asked. She saw Rubi as a sister-in-law, and she thought Rubi appeared to be out of it. "How'd you get home?"

In a somber voice, Rubi said, "*...it's my birthday!*"

Penelope knew something was different, but she couldn't put her finger on it. As she was following Rubi into her room, Rubi shut the door in her face.

As Penelope was about to shoot a cuss word, the door opened, and Rubi snatched Penelope by the arm into the room. "I'm okay," Rubi told her.

Penelope plopped down on the bed and said, "If you say so. But if there's anything you want to talk about, you know I'm always here for you."

Rubi stripped down in front of Penelope, something she'd never done before, then started shooting orders, "Have my nail tech here in thirty minutes. Make sure my makeup artist is here too, right after that. And, I want you to pick out the sluttiest skirt I own, in my closet, shoes to go with it too."

And with that, Rubi entered the bathroom adjoined to her bedroom.

CHAPTER SEVEN

Colombo and Carpenter were at the top of their games, as far as law enforcement goes, and they were doing it in a town Frank Rizzo made infamous for underhanded tactics that always produced results. Frank Rizzo's reign as top cop ran through the sixties and seventies. And his aspirations didn't just stop at commissioner. He went on to become Mayor of Philadelphia.

Every so often, as Colombo and Carpenter came to and left work, the longtime partners would take a glorifying glare, or a sneak peek, at the infamous Frank Rizzo statue.

He was a bad man, instilled fear, especially in the black communities, but he got results, Carpenter would often say to himself.

On the other hand, no matter how many people he hurt, no matter how many times he was sued for promoting systemic racism, Colombo thought Rizzo's legacy wasn't glorified enough.

Both detectives were white men in their fifties, devoted to the notion of law and order, superior to their peers, and had no intentions of seeking pension anytime soon. They'd worked patrol, narcotics, gang intelligence, organized crime, and now *homicide*.

Then why were they looking to interview Mes'siyah? Avery Trap was alive and well, which meant it wasn't a homicide case.

They were chasing the big one! That's why. And couldn't wait to sit down across from Bishop King's son, and heir apparent.

The dark inconspicuous vehicle they were traveling in was parked in downtown Philly as they watched the college kids blend with the notables, while gaining entry into the ballroom. It was a sight to see. Luxurious car produced in foreign countries were filling the adjacent parking lot. Fabulously dressed women and dapper men meandered outside before eventually going inside.

"There's Bishop King," Colombo told his partner. He was the aggressor of the two. With a paunch for a stomach and a head full of white hair to match his brows and mustache, Colombo stared intently.

Carpenter had managed to preserve his appearance, looking more like 45, than 54. He had fleck of gray in his curly brown locks, with a gangly physique. At 6'1", he was a bit taller than Colombo, but not by much.

"And there's the birthday girl," Carpenter stated, checking out how hot Rubi looked that evening.

The skirt Penelope had picked out for Rubi was amazingly slutty. It was designed by Versace, and kind of reminded people of the dress JLo had worn to the MTV Video Music Awards. Only, Rubi's was red with gold roses, and a lot shorter. Rubi's pussy lips would be showing if she slipped and fell. And although she knew she wouldn't be able to maneuver those bowlegs in the five inch Gucci stilettos, Rubi still wore them.

They were open toe, with rich gold links as the straps. Her nails were red, *the ones on her hands and the ones on her toes*. She swept her hair up into a gracious bun that held a bit of frizz that made it look exotic.

No one could keep their eyes off her celestial body.

Then came the booming voice—"Make way! Part like the Red Sea, please!"

The voice belonged to her cousin Big Body. He had been hired to do security detail for Rubi's birthday bash. He was trying to create a crease from the back of the lobby leading to the elevator up front.

"Right this way, Rubi!" he shouted, directing.

Rubi so elegantly followed his lead. The party was on the top floor. Inside the elevator was a mirror where Rubi caught a glimpse of herself.

"The red lipstick is setting everything off," she said, nodding her head and whatnot. "Eyebrows on fleek!"

Big Body was scrolling through his phone, and wiping sweat from his temples. He was a big man who had squeezed his three hundred pound ass into some white skinny jeans and a white fitted shirt.

Bish had beat them upstairs, and was off to the side talking to Rubi's whole student body of the past. Well, the peculiar ones who wanted to become powerful and successful like they envisioned him.

But when they saw Rubi, they clapped and cheered for their rich friend. The DJ immediately played RiRi

& Chris Brown's smash hit, *Birthday Cake!*
"*Cake! Cake! Cake! Cake!*"

Rubi was smiling, her diamonds were glistening, and she inwardly thanked her mother for putting it together on such short notice. The slutty look had been to create an uproar, but also to piss her parents off. It was supposed to be like when Janet Jackson had her revolution. But after seeing the staff who'd served her for several years of her life, and how well her mother had done, she somewhat regretted not going with the original choice which was sultry but a lot less revealing. But what was done was done.

Rubi began to dance, hi-fiving her friends, while holding her Carolina Herrera clutch tightly in her left hand. The lights were dimmed, the music was booming, and Rubi was high. She had decided to hit the toochie again, just this time she only took half of the pulls she had the first time. And she wasn't out of her mind.

Mes'siyah, who sat alone, noticed something was different about his sister.

Bish, who sat with immaculate posture, noticed it too. His hard bottoms were firmly planted on the floor, but his eyes were on his family. They bounced from Angel, to Mes'siyah, to Rubi.

Imani, Rubi's best friend, danced in a sexy shimmy towards Rubi. Everything she was wearing was made by *7 For All Mankind*. The skirt and the tube-top. She was super thick, big tits, big ass, flat stomach, and killing her outfit. In her flat thong sandals, she was still taller than Rubi. The two embraced; immediately Imani saw something was different about her bestie.

Imani could also smell what appeared to be a burnt clip coming from Rubi's purse. Rubi had a half of blunt of K2 in her purse, right next to her clear red Bic lighter.

With one arm draped over Imani, Mes'siyah gifted Rubi with the solid gold tiara, diamonds and rubies flowing all through it. "Happy birthday, sis. I know I be hard on ya ass sometimes, but it's only because I gotta protect you. The streets will swallow you whole if we ain't careful." He came off real smooth, nice undertone that brought a smile to Imani's face. She had always had a crush on Mes'siyah.

Rubi said, "Clearly, you be doing the most. And I wish you'd miss me with that shit. This my pussy, and if I wanna give it to a guy, *that's what I'm gonna do...*"

Only the three of them could hear her, but by the look on Mes'siyah's face you would've thought they entire ballroom had heard Rubi. She didn't raise her voice, just was very deliberate in her delivery, something Mes'siyah wasn't used to.

Rubi went on to say, "Protected wasn't what I felt when you slapped me around. I felt violated. Just so you know. See ya around."

Imani didn't know that Mes'siyah had put his hands on Rubi. And Rubi had purposely not told her. Now the cat was out the bag. Mes'siyah didn't exactly feel like shit, but he didn't feel good either. About the thrashing, or about how his sister had spoken to him in relation to her female anatomy and what she would do with it when she felt like doing it.

Trap God had been to some parties in his day, and crashed a few too. But Rubi's bash was on another level. Not exactly Met Gala, or a *Vogue* party, but the decorum was close. He was checking out magnums of champagne, undoubtedly 20 of them, standing 2 feet tall. He estimated they cost about $2,000 apiece— *minimum*. Each bottle could fill thirty champagne flutes. The balloons were even exclusive. They were shaped like rubies with matching red ribbon attached to them, all hovering above at the ceiling.

The cake was crazy. *Red velvet!* And it was big enough to have a stripper hop out of it if that's what Rubi had wanted.

Trap God knew the Kings had the bag, and that old money from the early 2000's. But this scene solidified it. He was gonna try to put a baby in Rubi *tonight*.

Rubi hadn't noticed him yet, but he was watching her intently while she wrangled with Mes'siyah. The two of them still had a score to settle. Mes'siyah had shot his best homie in the shoulder on some unnecessary shit. Was just straight tripping. As Trap God was recalling the shooting incident that took place on his block up Kensington, he and Mes'siayh had locked eyes. They were about twenty feet apart, at least 30 unknowing and unsuspecting attendees separating them.

With squinted eyes, and furrowed brows, Mes'siyah was not gonna break the icy glare until Trap God did. *These two egotistical maniacs, infatuated with their reputations.*

Mes'siyah wanted to know what the fuck Trap God

was doing there?

And Trap God wanted to know what the fuck this skinny-ass pussy was looking at? He never, ever respected Mes'siyah's gangsta. *He respected the brand.* Bish really came from the mud, the slums of Philly, and Angel had a crazy story equally as triumphing. Their shit was documented. As far as Mes'siyah goes, Trap God saw him as the equivalent of a trust-fund baby.

And it must be noted, he dug the shit out of Rubi.

Mes'siyah was approaching Trap God with urgency, leaving Rubi to wonder, *had she won her motion for control*??? She didn't even think twice, never even looked to see where Mes'siyah had stormed off to.

Mes'siyah was moving on some real aggressive shit, knowing without his gun and his gang, he wasn't tough. But Angel got there first.

She said, "I'm not calling you *Trap God.* So what is your real name, young man?" She was looking up into his hazelnut eyes waiting for an answer.

Trap God was hip, his ear stayed to the streets, he stayed on the Gram, but seeing Angel pregnant was somehow different. She was really like a celebrity, but one that belonged to the streets, and not Hollywood.

The baby bump wasn't protruding, but it was evident a life was forming inside her. And she subconsciously kept reaching for and rubbing her belly. It subdued him, put Trap God in a semi-peaceful state. He said, "Malik Leonard, is my real name."

"Well, Malik, thank you for coming. I want you to

pop one of them bottles, and pour the first drink for my Rubi. Think you can do that for me?"

"More than likely," he said, flashing a charming smile for Angel to digest. But what she saw were the long jagged teeth of a hyena. Just nice, white, and straight. And noted that she would have to keep two eyes on him.

"Such a gentleman," she said, then turned in her new Gucci tennis shoes that went perfectly with her white pants suit and Gucci visor. She turned right into her firstborn's chest and new chain and pendant. "Son," she said sweetly while reaching up to touch the side of his face.

"Fuck is this bozo doing up in here talking to you about?" Mes'siyah immediately quizzed.

"Bozo??? Is you stupid???" Trap God shot back, swelling up.

The party had taken on a flow the DJ had hoped for, so no one was paying any attention to the Mexican standoff brewing.

Trap God had only brought one of his soldiers with him, and they were searched at the entrance for weapons, so they weren't strapped. And Mes'siyah's gang weren't invited. But Penelope seen the small commotion, and she started making her way over there.

"I told you to stay away from my sister, didn't I?"

Bishop took noticed too, and immediately thought that Trap God had to be the dude Rubi had gone to the hospital with to make a play of his artist, Avery Trap. So, he thought it would be fitting if Mes'siyah straightened the young punk out for trying to corrupt his daughter, and fuck with his money.

Angel said, "Son, I invited him. This is my event, for my daughter. Not yours.

"Is everything okay?" Penelope asked, with her hand in her pocket, on her mace canister. She did not play when it came to Mes'siyah.

More people were coming in by the droves. Beautiful women, well groomed young men, and even some local celebrities had finally arrived.

With venom in his words, Mes'siyah said, "Clearly, mommy. Clearly."

As he was walking off, Penelope caught up to him, and asked, "What's up? I have never seen you so upset."

"Come on, let's get the fuck out of here," he told Penelope, not knowing that Ivory had just made her entrance with her lady gang.

Trap God let out a sigh of relief, because he didn't really want to have to put the beatdown on Mes'siyah. He wanted to beat that pussy up between Mes'siyah's sister's legs. And now, he pretty much had the green light. He reached for his phone, a natural reaction when he gets flustered, only to remember Angel had banned phones from the event. So he went and grabbed one of the magnums, two flutes, and hauled it to Rubi.

Pop!

The bottle was now without a cork, and the champagne was flowing. Rubi was surprised to see Trap God.

"And to what do I owe this pleasure?" Rubi asked as she lifted her glass of bubbly to her lips which too looked like glass. That's how shiny her kisser was. Before Trap God could answer, she was checking him out. He was dressed nice, nothing out of the ordinary. He being fly is actually what initially caught her eye.

Finally, he said, "I'm here to celebrate with an eventual queen. Happy birthday, Rubi King." And with that, he sat the champagne down and he reached in his pocket and removed a small jewelry box. It was flat, black, and about five inches long.

"Another piece of jewelry," Rubi cooed, as she felt someone coming up behind her. It was Ivory Manning, the DA's daughter, who made Rubi's smile slowly vanish.

The Dragon Queen!, Rubi thought as she played nice by taking Ivory's hand. "Thank you for coming. But, my brother just left with his concubine."

With an uncanny eye for bullshit, Ivory replied, "Is that so? Well, I'm not here to see your brother. I'm here to wish you a happy birthday."

This gots to be the baddest white chick I have ever seen in my life, Trap God said to himself as he watched the two young baddies send verbal shots at one another.

Ivory's blonde mane was let down, her nails and hair were done, and she was wearing a splashy teal blue one-piece min-dress by *Dir'Me*, with some slamming heels on her feet. She looked like a star.

"In that case, thank you," Rubi shot back, before adding, "Did you bring a gift?"

"I certainly did. A gift card," Ivory told Rubi as she slipped it from her clutch.

The card had $500 on it, and was for a spa. Rubi thanked her, then told Trap God to pour Ivory and her girls a drink. While all that was going on, Rubi slipped into a bathroom stall and took a couple puff of her blunt. She felt like it gave her super powers. Made her think differently. And, added rationale where there once was none. No one seemed to notice, and she was able to blend right back in.

While all that was going on, Bish pulled down on Angel. "Is this the dude my daughter is dating now?"

"And, it is," Angel replied.

"You did a good job on such short notice."

"I have to put out another image to juxtapose with the one the haters are putting out there."

"They want to sit down with Mes'siyah, you know that right?"

Angel looked up into Bish's eyes, and did not like what was staring back at her. She saw fear. She saw self-preservation. "My son will not be sitting down with the police. And what for anyway?"

"Some questions, concerning the Avery Trap shooting. That's all."

"*Avery Trap*. Hmmm. Her getting shot wasn't such a bad thing," Angel said, taking the intensity out of her stare. "Streams are up. People seem to sympathize with *victims who have popularity*."

Bish couldn't believe what he'd just heard his wife say. Was it that foul? Or, was it that she had something scathing to say about his potential mistress? Whatever the case, Bish was fuming. But sure not to tip on himself, he said, "Maybe we need to get more of our artists shot, and more often, huh?"

Angel cackled a little, then said, "I wouldn't go that far. Just the ones who aren't bringing in any revenue."

Bish said, "Now, back to business. If we don't let Mes'siyah sit down with these folks, it could jeopardize everything we built."

"But if they knew something, then why would they be trying to arrange a sit down?"

"Important people were out there, very important people. And, our names are dead smack in the middle of it, since Mes'siyah planned the event."

Angel, didn't disagree, but neither did she concur. She, instead, said, "Any word on Smally G? And that half million dollars?"

"Nothing yet. Although I did hear he was making funeral arrangements for his dead mother. What a sweet lady she was."

There wasn't much Bish did that Angel didn't know about. "Well, in that case, I say we make arrangements for our son to talk to those slimy police."

As Bish was about to reclaim his seat, Angel grabbed his hand, said, "Gimme kiss, poppa. You been acting real funny too. Let me find out, you getting soft."

The two smooched, catching the eye of their staff, whom all began to clap to make a showing of solidarity within the unit. *And that it did.*

The very few who were allowed to carry their phones,

were posting the shot of the Kings kissing on their blogs and various platforms.

On the other hand, the smoke was playing tricks on Rubi again. She was watching her parents thinking of how much fun it would be for her and her man to take the throne.

Bish used the moment to ask Angel, "How much do you think we're worth right now? All of our assets?"

"Last I checked, twenty-five million," Angel said, with poked out lips for another kiss.

Rubi, who was right across the ballroom watching them, estimated their worth to be at $100,000,000. *Kids! What do they know?* What Rubi knew for sure was, that growing up, she was a sheltered child, never struggled, and that her parents were definitely rich, and that they had a butler, maids, groundskeepers, a chef, and security at their mansion. All of whom were standing together at her birthday party, something that had never happened before.

Angel said, *and Rubi was reading her lips*, "Between the recording label, the clothing line, the car dealerships, and our properties, I say easily we're worth that. Now, I'm not counting the street money."

Bish tallied that at $3,000 off every brick they move. And they'd been doing a hundred every other week for countless years. "It may be time to put the streets of Philadelphia in our rearview for good, Angel. Before something really bad happens," he said, taking Angel into his arms.

"Anything on the home we're supposed to be moving

into in Calabasas?" Angel asked in response.

"Not yet. But I did speak with Thaila, and—"

"And???" she snidely interrupted. Make no mistake, Angel was the shit, and had put her life and liberty on the line to build what they had built too.

"—progress is being made."

"Well, holler at me about this when you got some more information on that. And remember, our baby is growing inside me. Oh, look who just showed up. Young Sheemi."

With that, Angel strutted off towards their young recording artist, *with the drip*. He and Avery Trap had a song *Wild Sexy* playing hour on the hour, and Angel thought it might be time for a video.

At that very moment, Bish wanted to be with Avery Trap in her time of need. He even thought that maybe entertaining the affair wasn't a bad thing.

I'm already having an emotional affair with her. Why not make it sexual?, he wondered briefly before his phone began to buzz.

It was Avery Trap.

A text! It read: MAN, U AIN'T LEAVING HER. KISS IS ON THE WORLD WIDE WEB.

Bish texted back: FOR THE PUBLIC.

Avery Trap texted back: ♪

Bish just smiled.

And Rubi was watching.

Father and daughter's eyes actually locked.

CHAPTER EIGHT

Colombo and Carpenter finally got a chance to meet the next generation of the King crime syndicate. It wasn't on the terms that they'd hoped for. But it was a start.

So, Mes'siyah had stormed out of Rubi's birthday bash, with this sensationally beautiful woman following closely in his footsteps. Almost in a docile manner too.

He jumped into a Chevy truck, two-door, and black. It wasn't just shiny, but it appeared to be oddly heavy. Of course, the wide body Blazer would be bigger than the base model. But this SUV moved different.

From a short distance, the two longtime colleagues tailed the truck. Mes'siyah was traveling through downtown Philadelphia like he owned it. And in Mes'siyah's mind, *he did own it*. He actually thought he ran the city.

In the passenger seat of the Chevy Blazer, Penelope rubbed her fingertips up and down Mes'siyah's crotch area in this wild seductive way that made him want her more. He hadn't fucked Penelope in a couple months. No dick sucks. Nothing!! To busy running the streets.

And, of course busy banging a bunch of other broads.

Without a clue that he was being followed, Mes'siyah told Penelope, "Take it out of my Balmain's, and put in ya mouth." His penis was hard and stiff and ready to be devoured so he could bust all in her waiting mouth. The prelude to a fuck fest between these two secret lovers that had been brewing for a while. What he also didn't notice was that he had run a red light.

Instantaneously, the overhead lights of their un-marked came on. Another patrol car joined the two detectives as Mes'siyah was pulling over from a busy intersection. The tints were so black that the police could not see inside. Mes'siyah only drove this vehicle when it was nighttime and when he wasn't with the gang.

Quickly, Mes'siyah zipped his jeans back up, and he and Penelope switched seats.

The son of a business mogul, he immediately called his parents and let them know he'd been stopped by cops. It was 2016, and unarmed black kids were being gunned down by police at a rapid pace in America. Mes'siyah wasn't taking any chances.

So it wasn't until he saw their shields, recognized the two detectives' faces from the news, that he let his guard and his window down. Like everyone else who entered his orbit, Mes'siyah thought they would be on his dick too. That's how much clout his family had, and twisted his thought process was.

For some reason, they weren't worried about Mes'siyah reaching for a weapon. They weren't worried about gunfire. So they told the two much younger white men in the patrol car to proceed, that everything was under control.

The next thing that was said was, "Turn off the engine. And sit the keys on the dash. Then, slowly step down out of the vehicle. Not you, ma'am, you Mr. Mes'siyah King."

Mes'siyah put his hands up, so they could be seen, while Penelope watched as she filled up with anxiety. Oddly, they never said another word to her.

On the sidewalk, both detectives introduced them-selves, then Carpenter said, "You shot through that—"

"I didn't shoot anybody," Mes'siyah immediately spat in his defense.

"—red light back there."

Both in plain clothes, Colombo and Carpenter, gave each other this knowing look.

"Where you in a rush to?" asked Colombo, with his head cocked to the side.

Carpenter was checking out the exterior of the vehicle. Now he understood why the SUV was moving rather oddly. *It was bulletproof.* That made it sig-nificantly heavier than it would have been without the enhancement.

"The light changed so fast. But, see, I wasn't driving, she was, so why ya'll asking me about that?" Mes'siyah said, defending himself.

Penelope was an *illegal*, entered the country as a young girl without any papers. So she was beginning to

65

panic a bit.

Mes'siyah expected them to ask for license and registration next, issue a citation, than send them on their way. But as midnight traffic continued to move on that summer night, nothing normal would follow.

"We've been trying to get you to sit down for questioning. We're looking into the matter of a singer being shot at your event, on the Fourth of July, year 2016. You were there that night, correct?"

"Hold the fuck up," Mes'siyah said in a low pitch.

"Someone made a statement on the record that you were there, and returned fire. You didn't hit anyone, thank God, but the shell casings, they were found at another shooting."

"You tell whoever said that to stop telling lies about me, and I'll stop telling the truth about them. Straight like that."

Colombo said, "What we want to know is, *was your father shooting?*"

"My father is a business, man. He ain't got no time to be in the streets wilding and whatnot," Mes'siyah replied. And there wasn't much wavering. But what he hadn't denounced was whether or not he was a shooter. But in the back of his mind, he couldn't help but think, *what fucking shell casings??? And who the fuck made a statement about me firing a stick???*

And both of those seasoned vets took note of that. The shell casings in question were found outside a papi store, on 27th and Croosky, where a 23-year-old Latina lay slain, three to the head.

Mes'siyah may've had the surveillance disc from that storefront murder, but his young boy Nico had left behind the shells. That was just one month prior to them being ambushed by Smally G. *June 4ᵗʰ, July 4ᵗʰ*.

Then he said, "I'm not a shooter, I'm not a witness, I don't give statements either. Maybe you should be talking to my friend, Avery Trap…"

And with that, Mes'siyah jumped back into the company vehicle, and said, "Ride, ma!"

"Fuck was that about?" Penelope asked off the rip.

"The girl who sings that song, *Wild Sexy*, they're investigating her shooting."

"*Whaaaa?*" Penelope said. Even she knew that didn't make sense. Being questioned about a shooting at a traffic stop, after dark. Then there was a traffic violation, which she was *almost* prepared to take the fall for, but no ticket was issued? "Are you serious?"

"I look like I'm fucking playing?"

Naïve was one thing, but to be slow was another. Penelope had been with this family for years, and there was nothing slow about her. She knew they were not squeaky clean, and that they weren't making enough music, selling enough cars, or restoring enough property to live the lifestyle they were living. But when she thought again, the *Dir'Me* clothing company was very competitive and fly, and selling online at all six boutiques, so it was possible.

Penelope had never seen any drugs or serious crimes codes being broken, but it was always in the back of her mind. *People weren't super nice to these people because they were nice people*, she would contemplate. And, that would heighten the allure.

With what she'd just witnessed, she could conclusively say that most of their businesses were just a cover for their illegal life. And just like that, her life had just changed. That's right! She would no longer just be taking orders, dusting and sweeping, waiting around to see if Mes'siyah noticed her today. All that shit was over. She was still going to do her job, because she loved it, working there at the mansion. But shit was definitely gonna be different.

"What are you doing?" Mes'siyah asked.

"Pulling over," she began, before looking over at him leeringly, and adding, "so you can drive."

"*Whaaaa?*" he said in her *very* Latina accent. More so, because he was shocked that she had spoken to him with so much sass, and definitely not to mock her.

"The Marriott. I want some dick, and I don't want anyone to hear me screaming. You are going to beat this pussy up tonight, Mes'siyah! You hear me???"

$ $ $

Smally G had rented a room in that same hotel. And he'd been waiting for hours for Rubi's return. He beginning to become furious because he had given her specific orders, *Now make sure you don't keep me waiting too long...*

Rubi had done exactly that. It was after three. She'd

been gone for hours. And he had been watching *Love & Hip Hop* on Demand, while puffing his *toochie* and eating hotel food. Now he wanted some of that fresh pussy. He wasn't into younger girls. Nah, no creepy shit. He had an ego, was power struck, but he wasn't narcissist or psychopathic like those wealthy privileged men who take advantage for prepubescent underage girls because they can't captivate grown women. *This was business.*

Only this business deal had taken an unforeseen turn. Rubi had been wowed by Trap God, and the $10,000 tennis bracelet he'd brought her for her birthday. So the two had gone to a secluded area, and they just talked. There, she realized, Trap God could be made to move to her beat. He would be a willing participant in her push to become queen. It was the drugs that had her opening up more, and she slipped and said, "Mes'siyah slapped the shit out of me, so hard, and, and my parents just sat there and watched. Like I wasn't shit. Can you believe that?"

Or was it a slip of the tongue???

Nevertheless, Trap God was furious. He took Rubi into his arms, wrapped his fingers and palms around her juicy ass, and said, "If that nigga ever puts his hands on my girl again, I will stab that nigga until my arm get tired."

Smally G may have said something as sinisterly charming, had she shared the abuse with him, but the almost insane high she was on just made it seem so romantic to her. *A man possibly killing her brother for her.*

"For real, Trap God?" she quizzed, all gushy and shit, then kissed his lips before he could even respond.

"Word to the hood, babygirl," he assured.

That night, the two danced the night away, with Bish wondering if it was Trap God who had accompanied Rubi to Avery Trap's hospital room when she tampered with his artist.

That night, Rubi also gave herself to Trap God. And that had been the first virgin he had ever deflowered. She didn't have any regrets, because she had already decided when, *and if,* the time came, she would tell Smally G he was her first too. *Straight like that.*

CHAPTER NINE

The party had gone off like fireworks, garnering the attention and publicity Angel had anticipated. And she could not have been happier. But the elation was short lived. She was livid when Mes'siyah began running down all the details of the traffic stop from the night before.

"Colombo and Carpenter?" she huffed, looking down at her fluffy and furry slippers with her white toenails peeping out of them. *Those are the same cops who had arrested Bishop and Smally G on those homicide charges back in the day*, Angel thought quickly. She had been just a block away, in a separate car, when the old cronies were apprehended.

"Mommy, these dudes look wicked. I thought they was gonna shoot me," he went on saying, knowing that was the farthest thing from the truth. The thought had crossed his mind, but it quickly vanished, like in the blink of an eye. He had actually expected them to try to shake him down. They didn't play fair, but they weren't on the take. They were into taking shit down.

"I'm sorry we didn't come out there when you called. But that's why you keep that phone on you, and keep that shit recording at all times.

"We had some *verrry* important people on the scene. And I'm trying to deflect all that bad press your Fourth of July block party brung this family."

Mes'siyah turned up his lips. "Important people like who, mom? Bunch of nobodies were up in there."

"Ivory came by with her girls."

Angel enjoyed the bewilderment on her child's face when she said that.

"Word???" Mes'siyah snapped, grazing his fluffy Philly beard with his right hand.

"The Present was there. He agreed to do the video shoot for Avery Trap and Young Sheemi's new single."

"That *Wild Sexy* shit?"

Angel and Mes'siyah were standing in the area of the house that separated the exquisite kitchen from the huge living room. Right beneath the chandelier and just a couple feet from the island top.

Just a few feet away from them, Rubi was sipping a glass of orange juice while listening to their conversation. Her antennas went up when she heard Avery Trap's name and *video shoot* in the same sentence. The Present was an up and coming music video producer. And he had actually hit on Rubi while at her party. In fact, he had cut in for one dance with the birthday girl while she and Trap God were doing their *two-step*.

Trap God! He had been blowing Rubi's phone up all morning. Done went and changed his status on all his social media. It no longer read: SINGLE.

He had hit it right, yeah, did it right, and Rubi had not one complaint for her first time. But, she had promised

Smally G she would accompany him down to Charleston, South Carolina for his mother's funeral. And after all, she wasn't committed to anyone.

She rested her butt up against the redwood countertop by the fridge, and continued to listen to her mother and brother talk.

"That's like really the first real hit under the record company," Mes'siyah said, now rubbing the deep dish waves in his dark hair. His shapeup was tight as always, and he was dripping in all Gucci attire.

Angel smacked him on his arm, said, "That's not true! There were others."

The truth of the matter is, prior to signing Avery Trap and Young Sheemi, the company, after taxes and paying their employees, was basically breaking even every year. The company name held value, but they weren't cranking out hit. They had got in the business a bit late, when the industry was changing from vinyl and cassette and compact discs to streaming. And their main focus wasn't to win awards and top the charts, but just to have another revenue stream. Now, they *really* had a hit on their hands.

"Name another one?" Mes'siyah said stuffing his hands in his pockets which were flush with cash.

"Be careful out there in those streets, please," she said, changing the topic. "Those two pieces of shit are the real deal. You didn't say anything out of pocket, did you?"

"Ma, is you serious?"

"I'm very serious. If you slip up, they will trip you."

"They asked about dad," Mes'siyah revealed. "They wanted to know was he shooting. And they saying they got a witness already saying they seen me squeezing."

Rubi's phone rang, making both Mes'siyah and Angel walk and look around the corner. By the time they got there, Rubi's back was to them and she was talking, acting as if she didn't notice them.

It was Smally G this time, not Trap God. He was ready to hit the road. So he could get back and show his ass. There was no way they were going to kill his mother, and shit wouldn't hit the fan.

When they were convinced that their conversation was exclusive, they turned on their heels and headed deeper in to the mansion where only they could talk.

On the other hand, Rubi told Smally G, "Something else has come up. I'm sorry, but I'm not going to be able to make it."

Smally G wanted to spaz on her, say some real foul shit, but his intelligence kicked in. So, he simply said, "It's cool, lil' mama."

"I'll make it up to you."

"How?"

"I don't know. But—"

"You left me with a hard dick. Never came back. And now you showing me, ya word taste like ass."

The thought of him tasting her ass, and her pussy, popped in her mind. Trap God didn't even sniff her down there, just straight slid into a Trojan then eased his way in until it was mad slippery and she was moaning and groaning and wailing and screaming.

"Don't say that, Charlie," Rubi said, acting as if she felt bad, when she really didn't give two fucks.

"You know what it means when someone says your words taste like ass?"

"No, sorry, but I don't."

Charlie said, "Ya word ain't shit. That's what that means."

"That's not gonna make me change my mind. I already told you, something came up."

Charlie hung up on her. He then called his baby moms and told her to call in sick, she would be traveling south with him for a few days. *Death in the family*. She quickly cashed in on her sick days.

Meanwhile, Rubi climbed into her new Porsche truck, and headed over to the hospital. When she got there she was told Avery Trap had checked out. In a high-step, she made her way back to the parking lot where she got on her phone.

Avery Trap was back in the Bronx, New York with her immediate family. She didn't even tell Bishop that she was leaving Philly. She just up and left.

But as soon as Rubi got Avery Trap on the phone, she said, "I was able to get a budget to do your first major video…booboo."

"What?" Avery Trap said, smiling. Her previous visual efforts for her music were above average but nothing to reach mainstream levels of the business.

"The Present, he was at my birthday bash last night, and he's on board. He's gonna direct the video for your hit song with Young Sheemi. But there is a catch. The

75

money is coming out of my pocket. If, you agree to become my first artist on my new management imprint." Rubi's excitement couldn't be missed.

"Did you discuss this with your parents?"

"I'm not asking you to leave the label, I'm asking you to become a star. You're bigger than this."

Rubi didn't realize what she was doing was out of pocket. She didn't know in that moment that she was about to write herself out of the will, for a brief moment of independence and utter rebellion. She also didn't know that Bishop and Angel was also calling Avery Trap while the two were on the phone negotiating.

"Hold on," Avery Trap told Rubi who was pulling out of the hospital parking lot.

Rubi held on, and Angel was now on the line, saying, "Arrangements have been made to take your single to the next level."

"Let me guess?" Avery Trap began, "A video, Mrs. King?"

"Yes, next week," Angel said, looking at Mes'siyah who was about to hit the streets and make his presence felt out there.

"For what song?" Avery Trap asked, not thinking that it could possibly be for the same song Rubi was just talking about. She also hoped it wasn't.

Angel said, "*Wild Sexy*. Here in Philly."

"I'm not doing the video in Philly. It has to be in New York," Avery made clear.

"Why not? And what do you mean?"

"I got shot in Philly. I'm cool on that scene. So, New

York, or nothing. Straight like that."

Angel couldn't believe this chick was making demands. *Before I picked you up, you was singing in subways during the day, and wiping tables at night in a seedy nightclub,* Angel thought to herself, sulking a bit.

Smirking, Mes'siyah left.

Angel didn't know what her son was thinking, but she rolled her eyes at him and said to Avery Trap, "I'm gonna have to discuss this with my husband." With that, Angel said, "Talk to you later."

Immediately, Avery Trap called Bish back. She said, "Hey. What's going on? I missed ya call."

"Why didn't you tell me you were leaving the hospital?" he quizzed, like he was her man.

"I didn't know I had to tell you I was uncomfortable and lonely, and that I wanted to see my family. Sorry for not telling you my every move."

There saw sarcasm dripping all over her words. But Bish wasn't surprised. Avery Trap wasn't a megastar, hell she was still scratching the surface, but in the face of all that, she still had a lot *drip*, as the youngsters called it these days. Never lacking in the confidence department, she spoke flowingly when she wanted to, and she spoke like she had a silver tongue when she needed to. And unlike Angel, Bish respected that.

"I'm coming to New York in the morning. See you then," he told her.

"I look forward to it," Avery Trap replied, smiling.

Rubi wasn't there when Avery Trap clicked back over. She just looked at the phone in disbelief.

BOOG DENIRO

A call from the big man, the wife, and his daughter within in minutes of each other???, she wondered, wandering barefoot and barely dressed around her spacious apartment on the upper west-side of Manhattan.

CHAPTER TEN

Mes'siyah made it to the driveway before he was stopped in his tracks by Penelope. She said, "When are you coming back?"

Mes'siyah said, "When I get tired of bringing pain."

"You ever think about moving, like getting out on your own?" she quizzed getting closer to him.

"Before I answer that, let me ask you a question?" Mes'siyah's lips were tight and curled in a bit.

They were outside and could hear some arguing going on back in the mansion. Mes'siyah got close to Penelope. This day, she wasn't wearing her uniform. It was very sunny out, and Penelope was showing a lot of skin in a scant tube skirt. Legs looked long and shiny in her peachy pumps, and her cleavage was glistening as well. Not to mention, her hair was let down too.

"It was only a question," she said, rolling her eyes a bit at no one in particular.

"Why aren't you dressed for work? You work here, you don't model here. Clearly, or unclearly?"

"Listen, I'm not in the mood for the third degree. I'm dressed like this because I am taking the day off. I been putting mad work in for this family around here. I think I deserve to be treated with some respect."

"If I wasn't in a rush, I would take you upstairs and fuck your brains out for talking to me like you crazy."

"Maybe that's what I want..." she snapped.

That Latin accent never got old to Mes'siyah. *Never!*

"I been thinking about moving out, getting my own place. Yeah, the thought crossed my mind," Mes'siyah told her, looking into her eyes. He cared deeply for the woman, but only saw her as a conquest, not a partner. He kissed her on the nose, then her lips, then hopped in his cherry red Bentley and only slowed up to let the gates open for him to leave the lavish property.

Bish was coming towards the front entrance, and the double doors that Penelope had just gone back through, with Angel not far behind. Penelope grabbed both of their eyes as she strutted pass them, not saying a word.

Upstairs, she immediately hopped online looking for a place for her and Mes'siyah.

Angel made a mental note to question Penelope about the way she was dressed, but continued to follow Bish as he shot through the double doors, then descended down the stairs.

"We built this together. Me and you. And if it wasn't for me, your ass would have been in prison. Don't you ever forget that!"

Bish had a small satchel in his right hand, and his phone in the other. They had been arguing about the money he gave Smally G. $500,000 went to Smally G as soon as he hit the city. It was supposed to smooth things over. But truth be told, it only emboldened him, which led to the silent murder of Smally G's mother.

The fact that Angel was pressing him about that was enough to run him off. *At least for a while.*

He looked back, because he truly loved the woman, and said, "I can't do this anymore. You got what you wanted, *another baby*, not let me get what I want. *I want out.* I can't do this anymore."

The head of the security staff, a retired military man, took notice to the fiery words and flailing arms. It was new to him, these two lovers, not on the same page.

Bish didn't stick around to hear anymore of Angel's self-gratifying claims. He went to the helipad and within minutes, the chopping sound, the whacking of the rotors, filled the air.

Angel called Mes'siyah.

By then, he was with his right hand man, Sacari, nicknamed after the Latin word *Sacario,* which meant assassin. At just twenty years of age, Sacari was a very dangerous dude, and loved Mes'siyah more than anything in the world.

He was saying to Mes'siyah, "A little birdie told me you got pulled over the other night."

"Clearly. But, you know, they gave me a ticket for running a red light and sent me on my way."

Sacari had seen the whole thing, and wondered why Mes'siyah had lied to him. He had planned on dropping in on Rubi's party uninvited, but saw Mes'siyah storm out the venue with Penelope. Instead of asking where he was going, he let the little baddie he had in the van with him suck him off, while he rode through the city not far behind Mes'siyah.

'Say no more," Sacari said, as he smoked from a Backwood he had stuffed with Granddaddy Kush. Sacari was albino, *like* straight white with reddish eyes, and looked scary. He wasn't really big, but had a big name in the streets. "Where we headed?"

"We gonna spin through 54th Street."

"And what?" Sacari asked, smoke pluming from his wide nostrils.

"Florence. Tell the guys to meet us there."

By the time they got to the 5500 block of Florence, three members of Mes'siyah's outfit were already on the scene. About six houses in, they saw six people out there occupying the curbside.

Mes'siyah saw a triple black Hellcat that sat behind an Audi, as he walked by. Sacari jogged up as he pulled out his Glock 380 with the 28-round drum in it. Nico, Sacari's sixteen-year-old brother, along with two other members walked through the lot to the driveway.

Mes'siyah scanned the driveway as he approached. Rico Havoc, a local talent, was laughing, arm draped over some chick with big breasts and wide hips, giving two dudes dap.

Smally G's brother, Mar, turned towards them laughing, still not noticing the threat approaching. But Rico Havoc did, and got ghost just like AZ had done Nas in the movie *Belly*.

By the time Smally G's little brother was looking back, Mes'siyah was coming down on him with a golden pistol.

Whaaaack!!!

"You pulled a pistol out on my mother, in NY?"

"Hol-hold...What the fuck?" Mar muttered, feeling as if he had been bludgeoned.

Angel was crafty. But she was also ruthless. While she had Mes'siyah's undivided attention, she told him about the run-in with Smally G and his little brother. She also told him that Mar might just be worth $500,000 to someone. So, Mes'siyah had extra motivation.

"Hold up, man??" Sacari said, pointing a Glock. And all hell broke loose.

Shots rang out from both sides of the street, from both factions. Mes'siyah and his men, and those loyal to Mar and Smally G wasn't backing down.

Philadelphia is one of the most dangerous cities in America, so there was no surprise to the residents of the Southwest neighborhood that shots were being fired with the sun at its zenith. And, as if prepared, or trained, the onlookers got low, while those in fear of stray shots made it back to their homes.

Meanwhile, Mes'siyah and Sacari were on their way back to the vehicle with Mar in their possession.

As they were racing off in this shiny ass red Bentley, Mes'siyah noticed a missed call from Angel.

"Yo, mommy," he said, breathing normal and with a leveled temperament. You'd never think he had a hostage in his trunk.

"Your father left here without telling me where he was going," Angel told her son, while looking at her manicured nails. She had the pointy new style that resembled claws. "He not the same man, I'm am telling you, son."

"Clearly," Mes'siyah said, doing the speed limit, just as cool and collected as he could be.

"I'm hurting, Siyah. My feelings are hurt."

"Well, I got something that might cheer you up. That tip, well it panned out."

"Okay. Your father doesn't need to know about this," Angel said, a smile widening on her face. "When are you coming home?"

"Listen, I been thinking about getting my own spot."

Angel didn't say anything. Her worse fear was being alone. She had an older sister, by two years. But back in the Bronx, she had grew up alone. They shared the same room as little girls, but they lived in their own worlds. Angel wanted to become the next superstar female rapper, and her sister wanted to be the next prom fiend. *Polar opposites.* While Angel's ambitions would eventually get her out the ghetto, her sister Tara would be mired in addiction. So once she started her own family, that's all that mattered to Angel.

"And when did you decide this?" she eventually asked Mes'siyah.

He sensed the *snottiness*, and said, "I love you, mom. We'll talk about this at a later date. Cool?"

"Well, when are you coming home?"

Angel sounded weak. Mes'siyah attributed the clinginess to the pregnancy and his father's absence. And that made him mad at his father.

"As soon as I'm finished with this..."

Angel had been smiling the whole damn time.

She knew her son. She knew him like the cuticles on her fingers. *True loyalty has no limits*.

As soon as Mes'siyah hung up with his mother, he had another call. Penelope said, "Twelve hundred footage, two bedrooms, two bathrooms, rooftop terrace. His and hers vanities. Custom wine cellar beneath the staircase..."

"What part of the city?" Mes'siyah asked her.

"Lansdowne..."

Mes'siyah felt a tap on his shoulder. Sacari was handing him a baby wipe. Mes'siyah had blood spatter on his white Gucci and the side of his neck. That meant Mar was bleeding in his trunk too.

"What's the tag?"

"Seven thousand a month..."

"Ai'ight—"

"Okay?"

"—let me think about it," Mes'siyah continued. He then blew her a kiss and ended the call.

Without even asking Sacari, Mes'siyah drove to Sacari's crib, where he grew up with his mother and younger brother Nico. There, they unloaded Mar, leaving his gagged and bound in the basement.

And like the true hooligans they were, they made Nico, a sixteen year old, hold it down while they went to get the car detailed.

After that, they went shopping, went out for manicures and pedicures, changed clothes and went to Club Onyx.

The sun had set, it was after ten, and no ransom call

had been made. Unbeknownst to Sacari, Mes'siyah had already planned this move. He was there to meet up with a new connect out of New York. Some Rican cats.

This was summer 2016, and Meek Mill wasn't the Criminal Justice Reform Activist he would become, a power move that would land him on CNN. He was a platinum selling artist with a girlfriend name Nicki Minaj. Doing a show in his city wasn't just a treat, it was a must.

And it was also not unusual for Mes'siyah and the gang to be in VIP. Strawberry Ciroc, Ace of Spade, and Moet Rose sat on ice waiting to be popped by the gang.

It was late July, but Future's "March Madness" was moving the crowd. Baddies were everywhere. Money was flowing. A bunch of networking was going down. Real diamonds, and fake jewelry sparkled everywhere.

Like he was St. Patrick in *Club Truth*, Mes'siyah scanned the crowd until he located Zion and Rushmore.

Mes'siyah expected them to have names like Javier, and Julio, be dressed like papis. These dudes were chubby off that beans and rice diet, and donned in the latest fashion. Balmain, YSL, and construction Timbs. *Yes, Timberlands in the summer. It was a New York thing.* So was the big thick Cuban links with the Jesus piece around their necks and hanging down to their dicks.

Mes'siyah also noticed Ivory Manning. She had her girl gang with her.

Mes'siyah with Sacari right behind him, made his way down to the dance floor, crept up on Ivory. She felt

Mes'siyah's lips on the side of her neck, and spun around into his lanky arms.

"Mes'siyah what are you doing?"

"What do you mean?"

Ivory said, "You got a girl. Your sister told me you left her party with the maid. Why are you putting your lips on me?"

"What???"

Had he forgotten??? This was the daughter of the District Attorney??? And simple assault was a crime??? Or that slapping his sister was domestic violence???

"Excuse me, Mes'siyah?"

"Nothing. What's good with you? Are we leaving together tonight?"

A pause. She looked to her girlfriends, and not one of them would have passed up the opportunity to spend the night with Mes'siyah King. So Ivory said, "I'll think about it…"

The night went on, the liquor was flowing, the ballers were balling, the stickup kids were plotting, the thots were thotting, the good girls were trying to avoid temptation, and Meek Mill was preparing to perform.

Mes'siyah kissed Ivory's cheek, and got back to balling. He walked up to Meek so he could be seen getting dap and a hug from the rap star. After that, Meek began to light it up. Mes'siyah rocked to two hits, then Rushmore and Zion made their way over to where Mes'siyah was posted up watching the show.

Rushmore ran things, while Zion, younger his brother commanded their army. They were from gangland, the Bronx. 183rd to be exact.

Immediately, Mes'siyah said, "You the nigga with the Coca Cola stamp on your product right? Like this is the eighties huh?"

"That's a fact, my guy," Rushmore said, in his Bronx New York accent.

Sacari said, "So what, ya'll niggas is like forty of something???"

The Mes'siyah's gang began to cackle as if getting older was funny. Mes'siyah kept a straight face, though he found some human in Sacari's sarcasm.

"White boys matter today, in the streets, I see," Zion shot back on some smooth shit. "I only know one white boy who name sound like something in the streets."

"My boy ain't white," Mes'siyah made clear. And Sacari wasn't. His pale complexion and funny colored eyes and the blonde strands of hair was because he was albino. "He ain't white."

"Well, that's a damn shame, he sound like a white boy," Zion followed up with, staring down on them.

Rushmore intervened, said, "We are here to discuss business. So, let's get to that so we can finish watching this nigga kill it on the stage."

Mes'siyah felt Rushmore's presence. It was undeniable. A force to be recognized. He didn't have to raise his voice to make a point. He spoke with sheer authority, and that was that. Almost in the fashion of a parent that operated like a disciplinarian.

The truth of the matter was, the level headed one of the two brothers knew these guys were responsible for the triple murder at the papi store on Croosky, but that Mes'siyah also moved work. They had done their due diligence, or as they say on the streets, *homework*, and made some demands before even entertaining the idea of supplying the Kings at all.

Rushmore said, "The cradle of American democracy. *Philly*. We're not here to throw insults back and forth, we're here to ensure the Coco Cola stamp represents longevity. And consistency."

Rushmore was a man amongst men. He didn't give himself the name. Nor had his brother given himself Zion. They were given the monikers by another New York Giant, who saw the two brothers as mountains. And mountains they were. Both stood tall and husky amongst the pantheon of dope bosses.

They would have preferred to be having this meeting with Bishop King, but the word was out that his son was running things. They got that directly from Mally Gz.

"I agree," Mes'siyah began, "we're not here to throw insults back and forth." Mes'siyah also felt like he had the advantage since they were in his city. And especially because he had let it be known that he was with the bullshit when they ran down on the papi store. Whether or not the Mountain Brothers had concrete info on the power move, Mes'siyah wasn't sure of. But he also didn't give a fuck. If he could secure this line, he could officially step out of his father's shadow.

On the other hand, if it didn't work, the two brothers would just make Mes'siyah disappear.

Rushmore's attention was taken from Mes'siyah when Rubi entered Club Onyx. Everyone was looking in her direction. Undoubtedly, she was worthy of the attention and praise her presence immediately commanded. And clearly, Mes'siyah was bothered by it.

He gave the Mountain Brothers some skin, then he and Sacari moved in the direction of the table that Ivory and her girls were standing around looking the part of uppity and boujee socialites.

He said, "What's up, you going home with me?"

To his surprise, Ivory Manning said, "Clearly..."

Rubi wasn't there to be watched by the hawks gawking and shit. She as there to meet up with the super dope videographer, Young Godd. He was quickly moving up the ranks, and not far from becoming a movie director. At 34-years of age, he only had two weaknesses. He loved fresh new pussy, and his second weakness was MILFs. *Mother's I'd Like to Fuck!*

Angel King, or Rubi King???

Was it really a question, deserving of an answer???

They were both incredible physical specimens, but Rubi was the new Angel. Angel was in her prime, already had her wings, while Rubi was on the rise, and with no mileage.

With his beard tight, not too fluffy, not too shadowy, mean lineup on it, Young Godd was in his own VIP booth where Rubi found him just lounging with the top two buttons on his shirt open, his dreads hanging.

"I'll do the video for you, not your mother, if you do something for me," she said, no charm, just went straight at it.

"And what might that be?" Rubi asked before smacking her lips and using those bowlegs to entice.

"Be my date for the BET Hip Hop Awards..."

"Deal..."

He reached in his pocket, pulled out a notepad. He was into all the gadgets, *i-this*, *i-that*, *android-this*, *android-that*, but handcocks were timeless.

"Write it down right here, then sign it. And I'll be in touch."

One step closer, Rubi thought as she penned:

I'll be your date for the BET Awards.

Then she signed it.

CHAPTER ELEVEN

Ivory didn't link up with Mes'siyah that night. He decided to tail his sister for a while to see what had gotten into her little ass. And after a few stops in the city, he veered off as she pulled up the gates of the Villanova mansion.

He had followed her to Kensington, where she met up with Trap God. Watched them kiss then part ways. He had followed her to a diner where she ate a breakfast platter alone while scrolling through her phone. After a while some dude, looking like he was almost twice her age and the streets hadn't been kind to him, came in and handed her what looked like a sandwich bag of incents. She slipped a couple bills under the table, waited until her new supplier left, then she did the same.

Once Rubi was secure in her bedroom, Mes'siyah watched her on surveillance. There were many secret cameras in clocks scattered throughout the mansion, and always recording. The oval office, where Bish conducted most of his business is where all the monitors were.

Now it was the next day, and Mes'siyah made sure Mar was secure before shooting out to the mall for some gifts. He got Angel a new Versace robe and matching house shoes, got Penelope a tennis bracelet, picked up some princess cut studs set in yellow gold for Ivory Manning, and didn't get Rubi anything. He couldn't believe she had spoken to him like he wasn't about to be the King of the Town. Or that she had told Ivory he left her party with the maid. *The nerve of her!*

Shooting up the winding stairs to the second story of the mansion, Mes'siyah now had some food in tow. He had always taken full advantage of the staff. Well, all expect the butler and the chauffeur. He liked driving through the city with all eyes on him. But the chefs, maids, security, he used them all.

The chef had prepared something special.

The warm body was still sleeping, right where he left it when he got there. He sat the standing tray on the bed and sat right next to the beauty. He used his pinkie to slide the golden lock from her face.

"Ivory," he whispered, caressing her long flowing mane. Her lids slowly slipped open to reveal aqua blue orbs. Before she could say anything, he kissed her lips. He then grabbed the breakfast tray and sat it before her.

Ivory Manning smiled, blushing, then said, "Good morning. All this for me?"

"Clearly…"

"Did you cook all this?" she asked, still smiling.

"Might as well say so. My house, my food."

"Are you always arrogant? Like, take no days off?"

"Clearly…"

"Well, that's not how it works. Because you pay the bills doesn't mean you cooked the food."

"Oh, really?"

"Clearly," Ivory said, grinning while trying the honey glazed turkey bacon. "O.M.G. Delicious," she sang as the flavors danced on her taste buds.

"You were snoring this morning, when I left out. You know that right?" Mes'siyah asked as the silk sheet slipped from her, revealing ripe pink nipples and tits.

Ivory said, "It's this bed! It's like sleeping on air."

"Siyah!" they both heard as the door was opening.

That had been the very first time Mes'siyah had ever brought a female home. The voice belonged to Angel, who also let herself into the room with her roaming eyes all over the place. In the nick of time, Ivory covered her breasts. Angel stopped from further entering the room. Gave Ivory enough time to get herself together.

"Mrs. King, good morning…"

"Ivory. How nice to see you, in my home," Angel shot back, wearing her new robe and house shoes, even though she was fully dressed beneath. She was not just happy to have received the gifts, but to also to see her son home, with a girl, and not moving out. Especially with Bish acting weird and whatnot.

"Clearly," Ivory said, and all three of them laughed.

94

"I'm a bit shocked because my son has never brought a girl in our home for a sleepover," Angel said, looking in Mes'siyah's direction. She had asked him not to do it in the past. Now, she didn't care. Just didn't want him to move out.

He looked at Ivory, and she smiled shyly. At that moment, she felt very special. "Wassup?" Mes'siyah asked both of them, his mother and Ivory.

"*Nothing*," they both said at the same time.

With one arm resting just above her baby bump, and her other hand on her chin, Angel said, "Are you two going exclusively?"

"Ah, we are in the neighborhood, but not there yet," was Ivory's response. When Angel left, Ivory further stated, "I'm a young adult, I wanted to have some fun, and you are fun, but there is a woman living under this roof who wants you too, and I cannot compete with that, nor will I compete for your attention."

"Clearly," Mes'siyah said as he pulled the sheet back down pass her breasts and took them in his hands. "In the neighborhood. I like that one, might have to add that to my lexicon..."

Angel didn't even say bye, just shut the door behind herself. When she got back to the master bed, she called Bish. The first time he didn't answer. The second time he did, and Angel said, "I was just in a good fucking mood—"

"But what?"

"—I have to call *my hub* two and three times to get you on the phone."

Bish said, "Wassup?"

"Our son has a girlfriend."

"Penelope, huh? They finally made the announcement, huh?"

"Everyone in the house know about those two. But I'm talking about Ivory Manning. District Attorney's daughter. She is in his bed right now, with little to nothing on..."

"At least this one makes sense."

"And you mean what by that?" Angel asked with wrinkles forming on her forehead.

"I wanted my daughter to end up with a man who can tell a fish fork from a salad fork, not some eight-ball shaving corner boy..."

"Excuse me??? He's a nice guy!" Angel boomed.

Bish said, "When I met you, you had excellent judgment, you were smart and you combined that with unusually elevated standards. Look at you now. Sometimes it feels like I don't even know you, Angel."

Those deep affective ties were most certainly dissipating. And they both knew it.

"Where the fuck are you Bishop King??? I bet you wouldn't say that to my face!"

"I'm in New York with our nephew, Mally Gz."

"I am telling you, if I find out you're in *my city* for

some other reason, there will be a price to pay."

"You tripping," Bish said, shaking his head.

"No, you're tripping. I'm fine. My son just came back from King of Prussia with this beautiful robe and matching slippers for his mother. I'm fine."

"Would you like me to bring you something back from *your city*?"

"No. I want you to stop getting smart with me. I am carrying your child, and I gave your ass two other ones."

Bish sighed. *Everything that goes right, and every-thing that goes wrong, will be tied to this baby.*

Angel didn't realize how loud she had become. "I just want you to listen."

"Okay, I'm listening," Bish assured.

"Ivory Manning is in Siyah's bed right now…topless, and grinning like she just had the time of her life…"

While Bish was on the other end of the line, Penelope had come up to make sure Angel was okay. So Bish wasn't the only person who knew Ivory was there. And Penelope caught the butt end… *"in Siyah's bed right now… topless, and grinning like she just had the time of her life…."*

The box containing her brand new tennis bracelet had slipped from Penelope's grasp. *She was beyond livid.* She had just fucked and sucked him until he could no longer cum. She had swallowed his spunk. She had let him splash in her face. She was just online looking for

97

a place for them to be together. But, she had never been in Mes'siyah's bed. Not even once, and they had been fucking for years. But, he had another bitch in there???

Penelope had to see this with her own eyes. Again, she was dressed down, not wearing her uniform, but something cute and revealing. So, she strutted down the long hall to the other side of the house, her Balenciaga open toe stilettoes *clickclacking* on the marble floors like she owned the place. Her long dark ponytail was swinging, she was moving fast, and brimming with jealousy.

In minutes she found herself at Mes'siyah's door. It was closed. She knew he'd most likely spaz if she opened it. *She did it anyway!* And strutted right in.

Gratifying giggles that only a thrilled woman could produce filled the airwaves. Mes'siyah was on top of and between the legs of what Penelope considered a *little girl*, kissing her bare chest, sucking neck, and tonguing lips. She could only see the small muscles in Mes'siyah's back, and just the side of his face. And then the sudden gasp that left Ivory's body made him turn around to see Penelope staring at them.

CHAPTER TWELVE

A few days later, Atlantic City

Gentle but generous moans floated from Rubi's vocal chords. The air had gotten thick.

Smally G was back from South Carolina, and he had his right hand pinching Rubi's nipples. His left one was jammed between her thighs popping her pussy. And all this felt so much better when Rubi was high. Her manicured fingers clutched the bed sheets as Smally G sucked the side of her neck.

"Let me know who pussy this is?" he had whispered in her ear, making her eyes pop open.

Rubi bit her bottom lip, curling her toes which were painted red just like her fingernails.

"Suck my toes, like you did that day in the Hellcat," she all but demanded.

Smally G's freaky ass slipped the toes on her right foot into his mouth. That was the shit that separated the boys from the men.

Rubi moaned in ecstasy, as she lay there her red-bone body totally naked. "Now suck this pussy, nigga," she said, making more demands. *And Smally G did it.*

While eating her out, he jammed his thumb in her butt, and she came just minutes after. It was nice and wet now, and she was letting out pants of invigoration.

Those kind of feelings were anew to Rubi. Extremely powerful, hard to assess. *Where had they come from???* She was in a haze, peaceful, thinking about ruling the world, when she felt Smally G's penis rubbing up against her outer labia. She released more panting as he slipped a couple inches in, then pulled back a little. The he started up again, this time four inches entered her wet pussy before he pulled back but never leaving the slippery canal.

"Put the whole thing in, and stop playing with me, please," she insisted with her head lifted up of the bed looking him dead in the face. "Yes, like...*that*..."

"Boom. Boom, booom, boooom," he said, adding sound effects to each stroke. "Bang, bang, bang..."

"Uh, uh, uhhh, hmm, hummm, hnnn, it's yours," Rubi told Smally G when he started speeding up to a stronger more powerful pace. She could feel him in her stomach, and his manhood filling her whole vagina out.

When she reached for the blunt filled with *toochie,* Smally G flipped her ass over. And took her from behind. Doggie style, he went to work, hitting it so hard, in less than a minute her head was bumping into

100

the headboard. He was about to come himself, so he pulled out, grabbed hold of the blunt, lit it up, took a pull and gave Rubi a shotgun like they were dude and Rihanna in that *We Found Love* video. Rubi sucked in the smoke streaming from his lips, then they kissed. He then advanced the blunt towards her waiting hand, but pulled it back.

"What are you doing?" she quizzed, eyes half mast, smirk on her lips, arm outstretched.

"Suck my dick first. You owe me. You know that right?" he told her, his eyes bouncing from the burning blunt, to her.

"I don't owe you anything," Rubi made clear. What they were smoking was hers. She'd found her own connect. But the look of Smally G's thick dick, glistening, pointing to the sky did something to her. If there was ever a time to start sucking dick, Rubi thought that was it. Two hands, she grabbed hold of his erection, moved closer, propped herself up on her knees so she could just lean in and start sucking him. But before doing that she ran her fingernails over his washboard abs while biting her bottom lip.

Smally G was high too. And he couldn't believe it was about to go down. *Angel hadn't even sucked his dick.*

Rubi's head, her lips, were descending. She stuck her tongue out, mouth agape, when Mar's ringtone spoiled the moment.

Smally G and Rubi both jumped.

The sound was jarring.

From The Bottom, by Meek Mill.

All action ceased.

"Mar-Mar, what's good? You never call, only text. What's good?"

"Shut the fuck up!"

Smally G's dick sent limp. His brows furrowed. And he said, "Yo, who is this?"

Rubi took the blunt from his hand and took too many pulls. She was out of her mind now. Just for a few minutes. She had collapsed back onto the bed, eyes hugging the ceiling fan.

"You there, bozo?" said the voice on the other end of Smally G's line.

Smally G had an iPhone too. The newest one. And in seconds a face popped up on the screen. Well, not a face, but a head covered by a black ski mask. "You know what it is; payback, pussy!"

"You bitch ass nigga! Where my brother at???"

Rubi was now up again, hazy, but propped up on her elbows. She thought she could recognize the voice. But truth be told, the voice didn't even matter. She didn't even know what was going on. She was ready to Suck her first dick, and move that off the bucket list.

Inside the bathroom, Smally G said, "I just buried my mother. Where is the fucking mercy???"

The caller said, "That wasn't our work, so I don't give a fuck about your lose. I want a half million if you ever wanna see this turkey again. You got til Friday! I'll be back in touch with the drop off addy!"

The line went dead.

A half mil??? That's all I got!, Smally G thought, shaking his head and sobbing. *And why that number???*

He thought he processed information better when he was high, so he took the rest of the blunt from Rubi who was laying on her back in a hazed state, and on Instagram. He smoked it all. Smoked until his fingers were burning. Smoked until he had gone nearly unconscious.

When he came to, Rubi was dressed and on her way out the door, heading to New York to get ready for Avery Trap's video shoot....

CHAPTER THIRTEEN

Mes'siyah was getting out the red Bentley on 57th and Pentridge. He had just returned from the dealership pricing the new Wraith. He had on some preach Chanel sneakers, listening to Sacari running down how the call had gone with Smally G. His Milano sweatsuit was hugging him showing off his thin built and his pockets were poking out from the mitts of money he was toting around.

In the streets, dudes didn't beef with Mes'siyah too much. They disappeared. Every single violator, or person in disagreement, went missing.

It wasn't the idea of homicide that worried the opps, it was knowing the body may never be recovered. *Advantage Mes'siyah!*

"So, the nigga held up in the basement. We feeding him puppy chow shaped like beef patties."

Sacari and Mes'siyah bust out laughing, bringing unwanted attention to them. He had all his chains on, five in total. You could barely see his fucking neck.

One of the folks to look their way was a little dude

about five, named Bolo.

Bolo crossed his arms over his tiny chest, said, "Cut me a check, big bro…"

The boy's mother, known in the neighborhood as Lil Mama, walked up in her coochie cutter shorts and a tiny tanktop, toes peeking out her Gucci slides, as she was trying to catch.

Mes'siyah spoke, and she said, "You looking cute today…"

Arrogantly, Mes'siyah said, "Clearly…"

She had expected a compliment back. Nope. No matter how bad a dame was, it wasn't happening. He did take her fingers into his hand, and blew her a kiss up under the summer sun. He also gave her five-year-old 2 hundred dollar bills. Yeah, he was stunting that day.

Moments after that, he was in Sacari's basement looking Mar in the eyes. All those unknowing people out front. And inside, in the basement, was a man on borrowed time.

On this day, he wasn't seated, he was suspended in the air by a support beam, washing machines and a drier sounding off to muffle any of his potential pleas for help.

"Nuts and dick all shriveled up, got sticking out. You tore up, boy," Mes'siyah said, as Mar was naked.

That wasn't the most pressing thing on Me'siyah's mind; it was closing the deal wit the Mountain Brothers.

He was thinking about Penelope too. He never wanted to hurt her. *Nah man, not her.*

Mar had been tortured too, to see if he had something in the stash. But he was popped, fronting like he was doing numbers. Didn't matter. Mes'siyah wanted that money for his mother.

Mes'siyah said, "What made you think you could pull out on my mother and not use it and live to tell the story, fool?"

"Nigga's gonna try us. They gonna think they can get some shit off, but what you not gonna do is run around talking about it," Mes'siyah went on saying, as he paced the spacious basement.

Sacari was hearing this for the first time. He had no idea that happened. He viewed Angel King as an aunt and would do anything for her, including lay the murder game down. So, out of nowhere, Sacari hauled off and slapped Mar with all his might.

Tears formed and fell from Mar's eyes. He for the first time wished Smally G had been denied parole. He was human, and going through a tough time he attributed to his brother.

"Where is he?" Mes'siyah asked, sure the kid was ready to talk.

In a brave and brazen move, Mar spit in Mes'siyah's direction. *Hawk-twa!*

It landed on the Milano jacket.

Mes'siyah removed the jacket, and on his waist was

the golden Dessert Eagles. He also had a tanktop on, showing off all his tattoos. Until that moment, Mar didn't know it was Mes'siyah. He had pulled a lot of guns on a lot of people that summer. And women were not exempt.

Mes'siyah grabbed hold of a plunger, pressed it up against Mar's anus. The stick got shorter and shorter, and Mar said, "Uuuuuuuggghh! Fuck!"

That was weird. But some more shit occurred. Sacari got a call that he put on speaker. The caller, a low level crew member said, "Yo, some nigga out here standing on the Bentley. Walking back and forth on the hood and the roof. Word up!"

Mes'siyah was livid. He broke the stick off in Mar's ass hole. *Snap!* And then darted up the stairs.

It was Smally G, in a bullet proof vest. He didn't know they had his brother, but he believed they had something to do with his mother's death. And drama was drama. *Might as well address all of it*, he thought.

A baby Uzi was in his hand, 50 shot clip sticking out the bottom.

Sixteen-year-old Nico came out the back of the house, made his way around front, gun aimed in Smally G's direction. Mes'siyah wanted that money back, but he couldn't have niggas violating like this idiot was.

Nico's braids were swinging an dos was the Glock 23 in his hand. Lil Mama grabbed her son just as Nico started squeezing the trigger.

107

The hood broke out into a frenzy. Sacari and Mes'siayh ran out of the alleyway as Smally raised the automatic weapon. He let that shit go.

Sacari pushed off the ground, having dove to the pavement for safety.

BOCKA! BOCKA! BOCKA! BOCKA!

The 380 projectiles slammed into Smally G's chest, knocking him clean off the Bentley.

The kid who made the call started popping at Smally G too. Smally G quickly backed him down, he was inexperienced in gun battle. Nico had holes in his Polo gear, but miraculously none in his bronze flesh.

Mes'siyah was stuck on stupid, for real for real. Not only did Smally G shoot the block up, stomp on his Bentley, but two innocent bystanders were tagged in the process.

The last thing he needed was that kind of heat.

But he had an idea. He had the Bentley moved, then slid up in Lil Mama's crib. "Listen, you gonna have to control the narrative. I wasn't out here today. Cool?"

Lil Mama was ghetto fabulous. A hood movie star. And a single mother looking for a sponsor. She said, "Bolo, upstairs. I'll call you when I'm done cooking."

"Can I watch South Park on Demand?" the little boy asked, marching up the steps.

"Sure…"

AS EXPECTED, 57th STREET was full of cop cars.

Mes'siyah was looking out the window. He also peeped Ms. Kourtney. And Colombo and Carpenter.

Lil Mama really had the upper hand now.

"You wasn't shooting, so you ain't got nothing to worry about," she said, sliding up behind Mes'siyah who was still peeking through the blinds in her window.

"My car is dead smack in the middle of this shit. And, that's the first thing that's gonna come up. That it was over my car. You smell me?"

Her nose was damn near up under his armpit, that's how close she was to him. "Yeah, I do. Old Spice…"

She kissed his shoulder with her plump lips, then showed him her tongue ring by sticking her tongue out.

Mes'siyah was a sex crazed freak, loved the attention of female admirers, but he could not take his eyes off the streets on the other side of those blinds.

Detective Carpenter, the taller and more fit of the two partnered lawmen, pulled out a *Staples* notepad and began jotting notes, when suddenly the sky parted and a downpour erupted. The neighborhood went from bright and sunny to dark and gray. The pounding of the thunder, the wickedness of the lightening, it was like a scene from a movie, as bodies raced to their respective vehicles and homes to keep from being soaked.

"I think I know who's telling on the block too," Lil Mama told Mes'siyah as he was slipping her from the constraints of her super tight and scant clothing.

…*Someone made a statement on the record that you*

*were there, and returned fire. You didn't hit anyone, thank God, but the shell casings, they were found at another location...*come to Mes'siyah's mind immediately. That had come directly from a cop.

"And who might that be?" he quizzed, taking his shirt off.

"First, how come you don't follow me on IG?"

"Profiles are like bathing suits. They show just enough to entice. You want me to follow you, you gotta be witty too. You heard...?"

Lil Mama said, "I been following you since you started your page."

Mes'siyah got the call that the Bentley was safe, parked up in a downtown garage, and that put his mind at ease. So he told Lil Mama, "You're gonna say I was with you, and while we were being adults, my car was stolen."

"The Bentley?"

"The Bentley. I'm getting the Wraith."

Boss talk always got Lil Mama's pussy wet. Mes'siyah wasn't really her type, he kind of reminded her of Snoop Dogg, his build, not his facial features. She usually went for fit dudes. But, hey, Mes'siyah was a catch too.

Lil Mama put you in the mind of Amber Rose, but instead of the blond lowcut, Lil Mama had long and near braids. Like Janet in *Poetic Justice*.

He pulled his penis out, said, "You got some rubbers

in here, right?

"And I do…" she said, licking her lips and bouncing that ass while her tits jumped a little too.

She came back, rolled the rubber onto his engorged member, then said, "The sexual thing is free. My potential and favorable statement is free. But, the info I have is gonna cost you."

"That shit ain't about nothing."

"Oh, and, if you can, get me a spot in that new music video. That would be dope."

"What video?" he asked, while tasting her pierced nipples. "Hell you talking about?"

"You sis. Avery Trap. She posted something about the shoot going down in New York, this weekend."

He kissed the black butterfly tat around her navel, said, "You know what else'll be dope?"

What?" she said, running her pointy pink nails over his wavy head as he continued to kiss her flat stomach.

"This dick in ya mouth," he looked and said.

So while Mes'siyah bent Lil Mama up, pounded her out, fucked her mouth and every hole, the two innocent bystanders Smally G shot were being treated for flesh wounds and questioned.

Mes'siyah and Lil Mama both enjoyed the session, then Lil Mama said, "Miss Kourtney…that's who's reporting shit that happens in the hood…"

CHAPTER THIRTEEN

Amy Ruth's, New York City

Potato salad, collard greens, fried chicken filled their plates. In their glasses was Sunshine—lemonade, fruit punch and a hint of orange juice—a staple at the establishment.

They all had the exact same thing. Rubi, Avery Trap, Young Godd, and Mally Gz.

Before dinner, they had gone to this spot called the Red Rooster for drinks to unwind. The place was very laid back, with the feel of the early 1940's, that wonderment time in Harlem. Everyone was dressed nice, even the white folk seated at the bar. And no rap music. On this day, Nina Simone was showing her vocal range.

Avery Trap was vibing, feeling the whole ambiance. More importantly, she felt very important.

Rubi told her, "You're glowing…"

"Good dick will make a girl glow," was Avery Trap's response, and right into Rubi's ear. It was between the two of them. Rubi just looked at her and wondered.

The purpose of the power meeting was to sign contracts, and lay out the treatment for the video. The only person missing was Young Sheemi, Avery Trap's collaborator. That was because he wasn't represented by or signed to Rubi's new management company— Red Rubi LLC. He was managed by her parents.

Avery Trap had Bish's blessing to sign with Rubi. He had took the copter to New York to let her know in person that if she felt this would advance her career, he supported the move.

Mally Gz was on the move with them because he had the connections in the Rotten Apple. Studios, exotic dancers, bottle girls, goons, gangbangers, club owners, and even a couple of MC's. *The boy was connected.*

So, arrangements were made for a verse, eight bars, to be laid in efforts to do a remix version that wouldn't include Young Sheemi, or delay production. After all, it was the visual that mattered at the moment, and Avery Trap the world wanted to see.

As they were leaving Amy Ruth's, a black Suburban pulled up. It was Young Sheemi, and his little entourage. "I ain't know this was a big budget joint, directed by Young Godd!" Young Sheemi eloquently put it, as they congregated on the Manhattan sidewalk.

Rubi had almost a half million of her own money in the back. She gave Avery Trap $60,000 to sign with her, and told her she would be on the red carpet at the

BET Hip Hop Awards getting mad exposure. She also paid travel fees, and for the suite at the Ritz Young Godd had requested. Without their agreement in place, to be his date, Rubi would have had to pay the Present $60,000. And wouldn't have had the trump card...*red carpet access.*

So, it worked out.

$ $ $

A hundred and fifty miles down I-95, back in Philly, a mother was returning home from a long days work at the hospital. It was just a little before midnight.

"Scottie!" she hollered. "I know you don't have no doggone dog in my basement???"

She sat her purse down, sat her umbrella down too, then called out, "Nicolas!"

She went to the door that led to the basement, when she didn't get a response from either of her boys. The sixteen-year-old, or the twenty-year-old.

She turned the lights on, and slowly took one step at a time. She was scared of dogs. And her boys knew that.

"What the hell???" she sulked, coming down the steps a bit faster now. The whimpering became clearer. *It was human not canine.* She stopped dead in her tracks when she saw the naked man, bound, gagged, and suspended in the air.

114

Not thinking, or maybe she was, she ran upstairs and retrieved a steak knife, one of the expensive ones. She ran back down to the basement and cut him down, after stepping up on a stool. The second he hit the pavement with a thud, she cut him feet loose.

In one swift motion, Mar ripped the duct tape from his mouth. He was scared to death, and could not believe his luck, so he just took off right up the stairs he watched her come down.

The lady was in this catatonic state that froze her. So a couple of minutes passed before she went back up the stairs. When she did, she ran to the kitchen where she noticed her favorite coat was gone, the keys to her 2007 Nissan Altima. The money in her wallet was also gone. She ran to the window, looked out just in time to see her car pulling away from the curb.

On the other side of that same street, Mes'siyah was watching the car take off like a bat out of hell. And he couldn't believe his eyes.

Within minutes, he was receiving a call from Sacari and Nico confirming what he swore he saw.

Both of them had been contacted by their mother, Kourtney Creston, who was hysterical. She went off about Sacari and Nico having a man tied up in her basement. They were able to calm her down, and convince her to not panic any more than she already had. But she kicked them both out.

Mes'siyah was shocked. Less than an hour before

that, Lil Mama said, "Ms. Kourtney is the one who gave the cops a statement." Now Ms. Kourtney had released a captor, and was threatening to alert the authorities if her sons weren't out from under her roof immediately.

The next day, Mes'siyah got the call from the Mountain Brothers. Which meant the Texas Mexicans were out, and New York was in. He called Bish to put him on, but Bish said, "The streets is talking. My phone is a call away from catching on fire..."

Mes'siyah was riding with $1,800,000 in the trunk of a cranberry XJ8 Jaguar. The Bentley was out in York, on fire, waiting to be covered by the insurance company. But the city was still talking about the masked man with the Teflon vest doing the rain dance on the Bentley.

Mes'siyah thought about blow-back that would bring. Smally G had really made his presence felt, and Mar was on the loose.

"It might be time to bring Whispers in, son," he heard Bish saying after about three minutes went by without a word being said.

And then the words left his mouth, as his grip tightened around the steering wheel. They went, "You ain't running this family no more. I am. Fuck you talking about, old head?"

"Young boy!" Bish shot back, looking at the phone as if Mes'siyah was there. But his battery had died. Anyone in the game with true connections was giving

Bish their version, their insight, their honest opinions. *Made men! Fellow millionaires who made their money on the streets.*

"Give me ya phone, baby," Bish said, quickly dialing back out.

Mes'siyah's phone buzzed, and AVERY TRAP came up as the caller.

"Ahh, that's why you fronting on my moms??? You done went and got you some young pussy, some young lips, and a young butt hole to spit in, old head..."

He didn't say that to Bish, he said it to himself. But the thought made him pull over in the parking lot of TGIF. Smiling, Mes'siyah sent the call straight to voice mail. And just like he knew, Bish called again. He must have got a charger, because this call came from Bish's phone.

"Yo!"

"Don't you ever talk to me like that, you little mutha-fucka! I put you on! Niggas jack you in them streets because of the trail I blazed. You hear me, young boy?"

Mes'siyah snapped out of the mood he was in and came to the realization that hi pop was right. He had blazed the trail. But this was the next generation.

He said, "I got you. But don't worry about me, worry about your daughter. She meeting up with all types of strange men, doing whatever the fuck she want. I got this. We can see clearly from the mountains. If you get my drift."

Bish said, "That's all fine and dandy. But, main man ain't no slouch. And his flesh and blood is the mutha-fucking dog he's gonna walk with…"

My pops done got super soft, Mes'siyah said to himself looking around the parking lot.

Mally Gz is much more rationale, less emotional, and I gotta press the button now, before it's too late, Bish said to himself.

"Young boy!"

"Old head," Mes'siyah returned.

"I love you."

"Clearly…."

And like that, they went back to their own head space, both thinking about one another. Bish looked up at Avery Trap, *his head was in her lap*, and sighed.

Mes'siyah's mind went to Ms. Kourtney. And her having to go. Sacari was his main man, but she was a liability. He immediately got Penelope on the phone.

"Yes," she said, sounding all sad and shit.

"I miss you," he lied.

"You do???"

"Clearly. And, I think you should pull the trigger on that place you found for us to lay up in. Like A-sap."

Penelope was happy, but she was still pissed about seeing that white girl in his bed with no shirt on. She said, "I know a lot, but you treat me like I don't."

"And that means what?" He was holding the phone just inches from his mouth. "Yo!"

"I love you, that's it."

"Then take care of that. Let them know we bringing the money tomorrow."

That was the first time a chick had told Mes'siyah she loved him and he believed her. He was numb to emotions. And love was nothing but an emotion that led to weakness and disappointment. But this felt different. Yet, he had already set shit in motion with Ivory. She seemed more like the sure bet. Political ties. The complexion for the connection. Educated. His seeds would surely have a shot at the good life if shit ever hit the fan. And, if he was lucky, she could run interference on investigations.

Penelope, on the other hand, would pledge her allegiance to Mes'siyah, and sacrifice her life for him.

"For sure???"

"Yes, I'm sure. Love you too, ma," he told her.

They got the $7,000 a month pad out in Lansdowne, PA, strictly on the strength of Bish. They were denied, and Mes'siyah had to call the Realtor, Thaila, who swooped in and made it happen.

Sacari and Nico slid through and grabbed their things from the house they were raised in, their mother never once looking their way. She would be mad for a long time, if it were up to her. *A naked man held up in her basement while she worked her ass off???*

As soon as they were moved in, Sacari and Nico in one room, and Mes'siyah and Penelope in the other, he began plotting the hit on Ms. Kourtney. She not only told the police she saw him shooting, but she put a gun in his father's hand too.

Protect the throne!, was all he was thinking.

Not about Rubi and her video that was nearing 300,000 views overnight.

Not Angel and her mood swings.

Not Bish with his ailing bravado.

All he was thinking is, *Protect The Throne!*

CHAPTER FOURTEEN

Thaila had finally come through with the California home too. It wasn't Calabasas, wasn't Hollywood, but Baldwin Hills would be just fine. Angel was ready to get away from Philly for a while. It would give her time to get pass the backstabbing shit Rubi had done. Who did she think she was? Rubi was a trust fund baby. Never had a bad day. Never forced a free lunch down her throat. She didn't have to put out early to get ahead. She didn't have to take birth control at fourteen.

As Angel was packing her things, just some of the many pieces of designer clothing she owned, her phone rang.

It was Brook Burnside, her bestie.

As soon as she said "hello," Brook said, "I'm only thirty minutes from Baldwin Hills…"

"Cool."

"And I'm pregnant too…"

Angel wasn't excited.

This isn't how she thought the pregnancy would go. And, she only wanted one more chance to get it right.

Angel knew she had done a poor job raising Rubi and Mes'siyah. Her son was a gangster, a move she had endorsed, and her daughter hated her. Yes, Rubi didn't have to say it, just look at what she did. Yes, Rubi hated Angel Ross-King, the woman who carried her for nine months.

But Angel would not be defeated. She had come too far. From the ruthless streets of the Bronx, New York, to working the streets of Southwest Philly. From cold water flats, to million dollar mansions. And now she was about to break in another pricy pad on the west coast.

It was time to get away for a little while. Maybe they'd miss her.

Bish was on his side of the room packing up some things too. He was also thinking. Just the day before Mes'siyah had crossed a line that wasn't something light. It was borderline a challenge. And Bish knew it. Hell, he had challenged plenty of people in his day. He was still challenging people now. But this was for the family name, the goldmine, the fucking throne. And there could only be one King.

It had always been the plan to have a peaceful transition of power, *from the senior King to the junior King*, but never to be undermined.

Then there was his daughter invading his thoughts. *Shrewd*, was what he thought when Avery Trap showed him the contract Rubi had presented her with. *Shrewd*, just like her daddy.

But that was peanuts. Musicians are born every day. Empires are built once in a lifetime.

So, Bish had to put some things in motion. He had pulled down on Thaila, and sat in front of her until she had a house. He wanted Angel out of the way. She had too much influence. She wasn't' just his wife, and the mother of his children, Angel could make this happen. She had gangster mannerisms, and she had gangsters on speed dial. Muthafuckas who still wanted to get in her panties. And would kill for a piece of that pie. He didn't know her every move, just like she didn't know his. But he fared much better knowing she was busy on the west coast getting acclimated in a new mansion, instead of moping around the old one with too much time on her hands.

Mes'siyah thought his pops was getting soft, but Bish was really getting wiser. And they all had Smally G to thank for that.

Part of the deal with the Mountain Brothers was the Kings would be buying from them now. And, Bish would give them the car dealerships. He had some extra money laying around that Angel didn't know about, so he took that and paid for the home in Baldwin Hills, then told Angel he'd used the money from the dealerships to fund that.

The dealerships only held 200 vehicles, mostly American made, and only did well around income tax time. Banks and other financial institutions weren't giving out astronomic lines of credit to car buyers. And anything over $10,000 the managers of the dealerships were compelled to report it before proof of sale would go through. That was never fun, but it lasted while it was.

So, it was really one less endeavor he would have to concern himself with. Now they were down to the property restorations, *Dir'Me* clothing, and the record company.

Avery Trap was still their artist, but most comforting was that she was Bish's young girl. 28-years old, 24-years of age on stage. She made Bish feel young again, she respected his wisdom, she acknowledged his power, she even sucked his dick without him having to ask. Her world was not consumed with money or violence. She loved to create. And that was the allure. A young fresh creator, versus a seasoned and devious dictator.

Bish heard Angel say, "Bitch, you know I run this over here..."

And that made Bish comfortable about his infidelity. Essentially, he was pulling out a new canvas and painting a new map to nirvana. Yes, what he was in the midst of doing was art...

Meanwhile, his son, his progeny, the disrespectful muthafucka, was carrying out a mission.

"Go to the Philadelphia Premium Outlet. Look for a Lincoln Continental. Two black Navigators, and two Lincoln Towncars," Bish had just told Mes'siyah only an hour ago.

"Then what?"

"Give them the one-point-eight..."

124

"Clearly, old head."

"Clearly, young boy."

The two gave each other a bro hug, but the shit felt weird. Then Bish had shot up the winding staircase, and Mes'siyah shot out the double doors.

When Mes'siyah got to the Philadelphia Premium Outlets, the cars were there, Zion and Rushmore too.

Lil Mama wasn't the only person who thought Mes'siyah was built like Snoop Dogg. As Mes'siyah exited the bulletproof Blazer, all the papis said, "*Flllaaacito!*"

Mes'siyah did not like that. Not one bit. He was slim, but then there was the super skinny jeans and the *too-small* Gucci Tee that showed his entire build.

Then Rushmore gave the Kings more than they could handle, which left them with a tab of four million in the rear. The $1,800,000 was just to get the ball rolling.

As they shook hands, Mes'siyah grinned from ear to ear. Zion said, "Next time, you come to New York. *And*, from now on, you report to Mally Gz."

"What???"

"Your father knows everything. Take it up wit him."

And with that, the Lincoln convoy pulled off, leaving Mes'siyah with 220 pounds of coke to unload.

Any other dude would have had no problem with getting bricks wrapped in Coco Cola logo, looking like some shit from the 80's, on consignment. No more going down to Texas. The only problem he should've had was, he had to pick the product up on 27th and Croosky.

Remember that papi store???

They wanted Mes'siyah to remember their niece every time he made a fucking pick up.

Mes'siyah's problem was, he now had to report to his cousin...*Mally Gz...*

The advancement of our people...

"That half Rican muthafucka!" Mes'siyah said, referring to his cousin being half black, half Puerto Rican.

CHAPTER FIFTEEN

By August 2016, Avery Trap's music video with Young Sheemi had gone viral. Millions of views. Thousands of reposts. Several renditions popped up. It was insane.

So, the video had taken place in one of the hottest strip clubs in New York City. The streets outside the club were full of gangsters and hustlers, red bandanas were everywhere, exotic whips just rolling through. An orange sports car worth a quarter million bucks was one of them, and French Montana was behind the wheel, top down and all. How could he not show up? The video was in his neck of the woods. *The Boogie Down Bronx.*

Young Godd was able to capture the entire Bronx scene of East Tremont. And as if it was a big budget action flick.

Then inside, only bottle girls and exotic dancers were walking about in *Wild Sexy* bikinis, while Avery Trap sang her heart out. But in one of the frames, there was shot of the Mountain Brothers, as well as Mally Gz and his gangster unit. *The shit was lit!*

Wild sexy, wild niggahs wanna ride me...
Wild sexy, that's why they bitches wanna fight me...

Check with me, I got the recipe...
You know how I like my pizza - extra cheese...
Y'all know how I like my niggahs – extra G...
Get ya weight up, wild sexy...

Avery Trap had never sang that verse better. The lyrics had never resonated more. Never had she performed better. And, Avery Trap had never looked better.

The icing on the cake was when Rubi slid up by Avery Trap's side, and in front of Young Sheemi. Rubi had a *Wild Sexy* tanktop on, no bra, matching white tights that also said *Wild Sexy* in gold cursive down the side of the right leg. The tiara Mes'siyah had copped her for her birthday was properly placed over her low and sleek ponytail her diamond choker was glistening on her neck. Imagination went by the wayside, and gawking was encouraged.

Mad dudes was sliding in Rubi's DM's now, and she was getting a lot of requests from artists and new talent trying to sign with her management.

Trap God was on her top, and Smally G was on her heels. It was all too good to be true. She had truly come from out under the shadows of the family name.

Shows were being booked. And sold out. Small nightclubs, auditoriums, stuff like that. Avery Trap getting offer to tour with big names. Rubi was never home now. So when she found out her parents had left for Cali, that sat her down. In their absence, Mes'siyah thought he was really running things.

RED RUBI

Rubi had a girl's night. She missed her friends, after all the traveling with Avery Trap. She just wanted to sneak off, puff her toochie, then return and have some fun with them. The thing was, all her friends could tell she was on something other than earth grown kush.

The girls pretty much just did the smores things, with some of Nicki Minaj's Moscoto. Dressed up in nice teddies, posted pics on their social media, with the sound system playing some Jhane Aiko.

"So, dude got you on your business shit girl?" one of her friends said, crossing her bare feet one over the other as they sat around a bonfire.

"This was all me," Rubi made clear, but not defensively. "No nigga inspiring me..."

"Ever since you started talking to this dude, you are hardly ever available," another friend chimed in.

Smiling, Rubi said, "Not even close to the truth."

"How you expect us to feel?"

"If you was getting your pussy ate like me, you would be on your shit too. I'm becoming a woman, that's all," Rubi said with twelve eyeballs on her. She hadn't told any of her girls she gave it up to Trap God after her birthday bash, then fucked Smally G a few days later. She was sure they would not look at her the same. But she didn't feel bad about it either. She had two fly dudes checking for her.

"Do you even know this dude's real name?" Imani began. "His birthday? How old he is? Have you met his parents? Where does he work? Did he ask to meet your parents? Your brother? Does he know who your blood line is?"

"Imani, you was there when I met dude. Cut the bullshit, please. You're just tripping because he came at me, and not you," Rubi said, raising up from her lawn chair in her white silk number that showed everything but still left a little to the imagination.

"His is nice looking, but not my type. I like boyishly handsome features with the rugged edge. That man looks like he been though some shit," Imani said, then munched on a smores.

"His mother was murdered not too long ago. And he had to go to Charleston for the funeral. That's where he's really from," Rubi said. But she didn't know much else about *Mr. Pussy Eater*. Except that he was on parole. She had taken him to the parole office before.

Lala was one of Rubi's close friends from charter school, and they had become heavy text messengers since the birthday bash. She said, "In some cases, less is more. But not this one. He could kidnap you for your father's money. Or your brother's money."

That sent Rubi on tilt. "I got my own money. I have my company, bitches. And I know how to move in these streets..."

"You're not from the streets. You grew up here, in this castle. Protected. Sheltered. Your dad and your brother and your mom are from the streets. Not you."

"Get the fuck up! All you bitches!"

Rubi marched them to the movie theater in the basement. Before they were seated, on the big ass screen, Rubi had Avery Trap's next video about to play.

New single...*True & Living.* She and Avery Trap were surrounded by a bunch of Bronx dudes, all type of foreign cars too as Avery Trap sang a sexy tune. The picture wasn't as crispy as the first video done by Young Godd. But it was designed to bring street cred to Rubi's new brand.

The girls were blown away. They all knew who Mally Gz was, *Rubi's first cousin.* And he directed the video. Well, he took credit for it.

You know who wasn't blown away??? Mes'siyah.

And standing next to him, at the entry of the movie theater, was Penelope. She had an evil little smirk on her face. She knew all about Rubi's emancipation plans....

SHORTLY AFTER THE girls were asleep in the guest room, Rubi returned to her bedroom, and Mes'siyah started moving the huge duffel bags towards the waiting car out front.

And as instructed, the very first drop off went to Mally Gz. Four point two million. Only, Mes'siyah didn't make the trip. He sent Sacari and Nico.

And then, he went on that mission to handle Ms. Kourtney.

Before the zenith of the next sun, Ivory was pulling up to the mansion unannounced. And Penelope was right there to meet her when she got to the rounding driveway.

Yet again, Penelope was dressed down. Air Max, a tight pink woman's Nike track suit hugging her curves, and showing off her tones tummy.

"Who are you here to see?" Penelope asked, A-sap.

"Come on, you are you serious?" Ivory replied, not looking too shabby herself.

Penelope could not hide her disdain.

Ivory's pleasant smile slipped from her face when she realized she wasn't getting pass Penelope.

"Is there a problem? Because I don't' want any," Ivory made clear.

"Oh, no, you just the flavor of the month. You're not a problem. You are nothing special. That's the problem with you white people, you think you special. You know who's special???"

"And who might that be?"

"People like me. People who work for everything we have," Penelope told Ivory, face to face.

"Really?"

"Clearly. This is a special family. And everything they have, they worked for. And sometimes you have to protect people from themselves."

"You love him, don't you?" Ivory said, stepping back a bit.

"Clearly. And I am going to have his children..."

"He told you me, you were the maid. That day you found me in his arms, in his bed, being fed food prepared by a five star chef."

"He told you that???"

"In those exact words. The he kissed me."

Penelope said, "He didn't lie to you. And—"

"Penelope, is everything okay?" Rubi asked. She had

Just come through the double doors, and out onto the oval step. "Oh, the Dragon Queen is here..."

"Don't call me that..." Ivory said, pulling her purse close to her hip.

"Or what?" Rubi said, inching closer to Ivory. She didn't like Rubi because Mes'siyah liked her. Anything Mes'siyah liked, she hated. Except Penelope.

"You and your brother's concubine have a nice day. Don't even tell him I stopped by..." And with that, Ivory Manning zoomed up out of there in her Porsche.

Penelope looked to Rubi and asked, "What is a concubine?"

"One having a recognized social status in a household below that of a wifey..."

"Whaaaaa?" Penelope said in her thick Latina accent.

"We all knew for a while that you two were fucking. When I say a while, I mean years. But you were my big sis before that even started going down..."

Penelope blushed. "Oh. Didn't know. And, what about you, who is scratching your itch? The guy from the birthday party??? You should bring him by."

"It's nothing serious."

"So there' another boy?"

"Yup. Another man."

Truth be told, Penelope was like a mom too. So Rubi felt like she could tell her anything. And she decided to talk to her about Smally G. She told Penelope what Smally G was doing to her body, told her about the first encounter in the Hellcat. The language Rubi was using was so explicit, it made Penelope horny.

"...he sucked my toes, licked my ass hole, made me fuck my clothes up, that's how wet he had my pussy. And I run right into my mom after my sexual revolution, putting me and my mom further apart," Rubi had chimed as they sashayed their way back into the mansion, their arms interlaced. "His thumb was in my butt hole while he licked all over my opening and my clit, *OMG*..."

"In your bootay, while sucking all over you?"

"Clearly...." Rubi confirmed, nodding her head, and batting her lashes.

She had Penelope's pussy throbbing and moistening, the way she had detailed the encounter. "Your brother think he's too good to give up that kind of action, Rubi."

"It's something that just happens. You don't ask for it, it just goes down," Rubi said, like she was a sex-ologist. "He just did it. I think he was trying to turn my young ass out. And now, I always want it."

At the island, where Angel normally sat, they continued to chat. There Penelope said, "You should invite him over."

Rubi's brows raised. Her parents were gone, in their new home, about to have their new baby.

Penelope figured, *if Rubi could get her man in here, then she and Mes'siyah could start staying at their new place in Lansdowne.* She didn't mind Sacari and Nico being there, but Mes'siyah was hardly ever there.

That first night in the huge apartment, she heard the door open, and came out naked, in the flesh, but it wasn't Mes'siyah, it was his minions. At the mansion, she could never do stuff like that. Just surprise him with some pussy, or a dick suck. Everything there was done on the sly, had to be planned, and during the wee hours of the morning when all the staff and the family was resting. *Slide in, slide out of his room.* Once she dipped into the shower with him, and that was the closest she came to being caught in the act, because Angel just let herself in without knocking.

"If it's serious, I would invite him over," Penelope said one more time. Then she switched the topic. But, the seed was planted.

CHAPTER SIXTEEN

Nico took it harder than Sacari, because prior to Summer 2016, Nico was really a momma's boy. Their mother, Kourtney, was gone. She had died like the iconic singer Whitney Houston. Found just like the legendary singer, drowned in a tub of bath water. Mes'siyah had broken from his normal practices, while laying the murder game down. He didn't make her disappear. He wanted his boys to at least be able to give her a funeral, so he flooded her with opiods. *Well, actually he didn't do it.* Whispers took care of it. All he had to do was promise Whispers that he wouldn't be cut out because Bish had relocated to Baldwin Hills.

"Couple bricks for you, old head," Mes'siyah had said to Whispers, pushing the blocks wrapped in Coco Cola logo across the desk his father once sat behind.

Bricks were going for close to forty grand at the time. Election year, border patrol, the threat of a wall being built at the Mexico/U.S. border. This was really good for the old timer. His best homie, Bishop King, was a multimillionaire, but Whispers was just a six figure nigga. Twenty plus years in the game, and never reached a milli. That would be the fate for a lot of hustlers.

"Thank you, young gun," Whispers had told Mes'siyah, then went on to seduce Ms. Kourtney with his charming ways. The rest was history.

Whispers knew this young nigga was cold blooded if he could take his homie's momma out. But then again, he was Bish's son, and his was just repeating itself.

As if he had no involvement, Mes'siyah traveled with Sacari and Nico to have the body cremated. Right after her flesh was turned to ashes, Mes'siyah used their pain to his advantage. They went back to applying pressure, and putting bodies inside walls. And Nico became more vicious, more ruthless, more demented. Sometimes uncontrollable.

But what Mes'siyah never expected was, for the little nigga to fall head over hills for Lil Mama.

$ $ $

It was September 2, 2016, Nico had pulled up in the Kensington section of Philly. He was driving the new Lexus IS Sport. Pulling the emergency brake, the car skidded into an open parking spot on West Moralan Street. When he located the person he was looking for, he pulled the bag out.

"Doc!" Nico said, his voice loud and traveling like he'd grown up there. That was the anger constantly brewing inside him. "Yo, Doc!"

"I'm not playing with you," Lil Mama said with a little bit of sass. "You hear me, boy?"

He was on the phone with Lil Mama. "Clearly..."

"You better get your ass home. I'm not playing with you," she said, using her experience to overwhelm the young boy. She knew every horny young nigga wanted a sexpot in the crib waiting for him.

"I got you. You want butter pecan. And, Bolo wants cookies dough. I got this..." After just two fucks, Nico was sweet on her lil sexy ass.

"Remember me?" Trap God said, popping up out of nowhere. Nico didn't recall the dude. But he slapped Nico so hard with his gun, Nico wished he had.

Lil Mama could hear the assault going down. She could tell it was more than one, more than two, maybe three assailants. Her heart began to beat fast, like too fast, like it was gonna burst from her chest. *"...And tell that bitch Rubi I said hi..."*

They had taken the bag, ran his pockets, yapped his chain, then the heel of a crispy double sole Timberland came crashing down on the screen of Nico' iPhone.

BACK IN THE CRIB, Lil Mama kept calling Nico's phone. In a short period of time, the little horny bastard had grown on her. He fucked like an energized bunny, spent money on her, and was in her bed every night. Part of it was the void of that his mother left behind. *Just having a place to go, and knowing someone is expecting you.* That's what made him cling to her so quickly.

Whatever the case, he was hers now, and he was in grave danger. So she hit Mes'siyah in his DM's.

Mes'siyah didn't look at the message until the next day. He was laid up with Penelope in the mansion. It was the first time the two had openly displayed their affection. And the staff didn't take too kindly to it. The whispers immediately began.

By then, Nico was licking his wounds and shooting shit up. He started with the dude he was dropping the *quarter-of-a-key* to. Shot him in his back, his ass, and then up close and personal. *In the face.*

After that, he went out to Lansdowne, and got all his belongings, and took them to Lil Mama's crib, where he intended to heal up.

Meanwhile, Mes'siyah had breakfast made by a five star chef, then called Rubi and Penelope down to join him.

As they were loading their plates with all kinds of breakfast foods, Mes'siyah said, "Sacari's little brother got abused last night. They are really going through a hard time. So, I want to do something special for them. Any suggestions???"

Rubi didn't say anything. But Penelope said, "A vacation. Like send them to an *exotic iiiisland.*"

"Sounds good," he said, savoring the flavor of the smoked turkey bacon. "Now, the real reason I got you two here together." He sipped some fresh squeezed OJ, smacked his tongue at the taste of pulp. "The next time you two decide to become my spokesperson without me asking, I'ma beat both of yall asses."

Rubi didn't respond, didn't stop eating either. It didn't matter to her. The threat or his attitude. As far as she was concerned, he could go fuck himself. She was not worried about her brother. Not one bit.

She was thinking about what she was going to wear when she invited Smally G over to the mansion. She was wondering how long it would take to get to King of Prussia and back. She was thinking about meeting up with her *toochie* connect and spending $1,000 with him.

"You hear me, lil girl?"

Rubi just looked up, expressionless. And kept munching. *The food was world class.*

"I don't care about your new company, I don't care about your new connections, I don't care about none of that shit. With mommy and daddy on the west coast, what I say goes. Clearly, or unclearly???"

Penelope could feel the tension. And thought it was unnecessary. She decided to end it with, "You know what I was doing at nineteen? Cleaning up after people. Your sister has started her own company. That is amazing..."

"If she had done it on the *up-and-up*, I would have given her credit. But she did some backdoor, underhanded shit. Just like her father. You just like that nigga. That's why ya'll get along so well..."

"And you just like your mother, that's why you two get along so well..." Rubi returned then left. Not just the table, but the mansion.

As soon as she was heading to King of Prussia, Rubi called Smally G. He hadn't gotten a call from her in a while. He always had to hit her line. Her head was way up in the clouds. *Straight like that.*

At that very moment, Smally G was helping his baby mother out of her uniform. Her ass was so fat, she could

140

barely get the khakis up over it. Now he had her laid back on the bed, pulling the pant legs over her ankles and toes. She was one of those fiery Leo Latinas. And she knew that Smally G not answering his phone in front of her, was because it was another woman. She couldn't be but so upset, he had done 20 years in prison. And, she felt he deserved to play a little bit before settling down with her. Plus, he took care of his son. And he was helping nurse his brother back to health.

Mar had suffered two broken ribs, his rectum was violated, he had been starved, and force fed dog food, so he was in bad shape when he returned. But he was back! And Smally G didn't have to part way with any of his money. What Smally G didn't like was, Mar wasn't telling him who had grabbed him. And the reason why: *Mar wanted no more of their treachery.* He wished Smally G had been denied parole.

"You know, if not for your brother getting kidnapped and fucked up, your ass would not have slowed down for shit," she said, unbuttoning her shirt and tossing her tie to the side. "Now answer the damn thing, because whoever she is, she is not gonna stop calling until you do."

Smally G looked down on her, with a smirk, that said *shut the hell up.*

"It's probably that Rubi King chick..." Antonita added, as she rubbed her bare foot on Smally G's chin.

Antonita had given Smally G his only son. It just so

141

happned to be her only child too. Their son was a toddler, conceived inside a prison. While Smally G was incarcerated, she had given him access to the outside world too, risking her livelihood as a corrections officer in the process. *Oh, she had a say in things, and Smally G knew he had better been receptive.*

"I said answer it," she told him for the last time, rising up from the queen size bed in just a thong and a bra. Her body was amazing, in a mop room, and definitely in her Logan apartment.

Smally G took the call, and could not believe what he was hearing. He was so excited that he grabbed Antonita by her big juicy ass and pulled her to him so she could hear Rubi say, "...You can't miss it. It's the biggest mansion on this road...."

CHAPTER SEVENTEEN

Revenge is a meal best served hot in the hood, Mar was thinking as they pulled up to the King compound. He still hadn't told Smally G that Mes'siyah was behind his kidnapping. They had already lost their mother, they were outnumbered, and he saw them basically pursuing a death wish.

So just as quickly as the thought of striking back entered his mind, his jaw dropped at the sight of three armed guards approaching the gates, wearing all black tactical gear, and brandishing assault rifles.

"What the fuck?" Mar mouthed, as aim was taken at the Hellcat they were sitting in.

One more armed guard, a sniper, converged on them. Mar was shook, but Smally G wasn't really phased. He had heard the stories from the horse's mouth. He just had to see it to believe it.

The gates opened and they were surrounded.

"Let the window down. Then tell me what business you have here!"

Contrary to his little brother, Smally G's jaw just got

tight. His temples throbbed a little. And just for a split second, he was convinced he had walked into an ambush.

"Rubi set me up. She know who I really am," Mar heard Smally G muttering. "I caught feelings, that pussy so sweet and tight. Fuck."

"Windows down!"

"Wait! Wait! Wait," the armed guards heard coming from the oval shaped driveway. It was Rubi moving towards them, the sun setting behind her adding allure to her shapely silhouette.

Sergeant Watts turned to Rubi and as soon as she was close enough, said, "Do you know these men?"

Watts was ex-military, salt-and-pepper goatee, muscles on top of muscles. He's been with Bish for nearly a decade, being paid handsomely to keep intruders out. A million bucks to lock him and his team in, then a quarter million annually to the four man team.

Rubi said, "That's my boyfriend…"

Watts took another ganger, and immediately thought he was too old for Rubi. By a lot too. The build Smally G had, Watts knew took at least 10 to 15 years to put together. Unless he took shortcuts.

"Mes'siyah know you got a boyfriend?" Watts asked Rubi.

Rubi had been smoking that poison, so no one should be surprised that she said next, "If you dont' open this fucking gate, I'm going to tell my father, I caught ya ass out back, poolside watching me while massaging your dick."

That hadn't exactly happened like that. But Sergeant Watts had been eye fucking Rubi on the low for the last two years.

"Let them through," he ordered.

Smally G watched Rubi jog back up the long black asphalt before revving the motor. The Hellcat roared and shot up the driveway.

Penelope was watching the whole thing while sipping some Moscoto. "We are definitely out of here now."

While Watts was trying to get hold of Mes'siyah on the phone, Mes'siyah was with Nico. In Lil Mama's crib. He hated to have to tell Nico this...

"This kid is alive, and telling on you..."

Nico had his shirt off, joggers hanging down his butt, saying, "The law is on my side. He robbed me. So they can't charge me for shit."

"That's not how the law works. That actually is what they would use to establish intent on your part."

"Oh, so now you know the law? Cause you fucking the head DA's daughter???" Nico snapped.

Mes'siyah was relaxed, leaning on the same sofa he had fucked Lil Mama on just a month earlier. He could only imagine what she had done to twist his young boy's mind up??? To show Nico he was still his boss, Mes'siyah put his baby blue Chanel sneaker up on the coffee table. Mes'siyah also had on a baby blue bubble vest made by Chanel. Everything else he had on was black and *Dir'Me*.

"You going out to York, until we get a grip on things for you," he told Nico, calmly.

"I ain't going no muthafuckin where, old head."

Not far away, Lil Mama was sitting on the stairs, knees on her elbows, chin resting on her knuckles. She had heard it all. Everything Mes'siyah had said. But, she had heard it differently. She'd heard that Doc was in a coma. *So how did he finger Nico???*

She began to have regrets about telling Mes'siyah that Ms. Kourtney was telling shit. She didn't know for sure Mes'siyah that was the reason the woman's life was ended at 40-years old. But there was no questioning the motive.

She began to think more, maybe this could be her way out of the hell she'd grown up in. She shot to the bottom of the stairs, having remembered something from that night.

"Trap God!" she shouted, entering the living room.

Mes'siyah and Nico both looked up at her.

"I was on the phone with Nico and someone said, *tell Rubi Trap God said what's up...*"

"Hmmm," Mes'siyah said, looking at her. "You sure about that?"

She trotted off, her ass jiggling uncontrollably in her black tights. When she returned, she played back some of the recorded call.

146

Mes'siyah said, "Do you record all your calls?"

"I don't," she said, holding her phone tightly. "I only recorded this because I could hear the scuffling and I wasn't sure if I would ever see Nico again."

Nico could not contain the love that was over-whelming him as he watched his boo thang express how much he meant to her. He was sixteen, but he wasn't the average sixteen-year-old.

"Well, if we get to Trap God, we should be good."

Mes'siyah took his foot down, and looked at his manicure, before saying, "I'm gonna let you two love-birds get back to whatever I interrupted. I'm gonna have a word with my sister. She could very well be in danger."

The door closed behind Mes'siyah, Lil Mama exhaled, while Nico's paw's grabbed hold of Lil Mama's neck. "Why didn't I know about this first? You didn't think I should know you had some info???"

"Get off my momma!" her five-year-old son said, coming to her defense.

"I'm sorry. I'm just going through the motions."

She wrapped her arms around Nico, and said, "I know. But, you'll get through it. And going to York might not be a bad idea."

"I ain't going not no fucking York. We staying right here, in the city—me, you and my son. Come here, Bolo…"

The three hugged, and smiled at each other…

Meanwhile, Mes'siyah was barking up the wrong tree. "You gonna get that nigga killed..." he said, racing towards Villanova.

"What?" Rubi said, in a lazed utterance. "Hello?"

Mes'siyah had hung up. He was only twenty minutes away.

"What's up? You alright?" Smally G asked her.

"Oh shit, get up, get dressed." Rubi jumped up, grabbing Smally G by the arm. "One of the rats done told my brother I got a man in the house."

Smally G's nostrils flared. His mouth twisted up. He said, "I ain't running up out of here..."

"Charlie, please, get dressed. And come on. I don't know what I was thinking bringing you here in the first place," Rubi was saying, while tossing Smally G his underwear and his jeans.

"This is gonna be the second time you almost sucked my dick. At least, take care of that for me first..."

"He is coming now!!!"

Smally G thought of the 48 Laws of Power, the Trojan horse story, and figured if he got in one time, he could get in again. Dressed, he said, "They ain't stop making guns when they made his."

That statement made Rubi's wheels start turning. How did he know her brother played with guns???

Making her rounds, just floating like she was queen now, Penelope bent a corner and saw Mes'siyah's room door open. One step inside, she noticed some drawers had been opened and rummaged through. She noticed that the walk-in closet doors was wide open. She saw that the door on the bureau were also opened.

Penelope sat her wine glass down and began to investigate. That's when she saw Mar limping around, and deep in Mes'siyah's closet. He was turning the dial on the vault.

"What the fuck are you doing in my man's room???"

Mar was planning his exit from the city of Philly, that's what he was doing. The watch in his pocket was worth $60,000. And he had pocketed a few mitts that were very husky.

"Nothing," he began, "Had, had to use the bathroom. And I made a wrong turn. You know, like the movie, ma."

With manly strength, Penelope grabbed Mar by his arm and marched his ass on. She said, "Don't fucking call me *ma*! And get the fuck downstairs. Now!"

As she was marching Mar out, they ran into Rubi and Smally G.

"What's going on?" aksed Rubi.

"I just caught this dude in my man's room. They have to go now," Penelope explained, as she regretted telling Rubi to invite them over.

"Come on man, we out. And don't call me over her again, Rubi!" Smally G said, acting like he was upset.

She grabbed Smally G by his arm, said, "Don't even act like that. And don't ever bring him with you again."

Rubi was just stuck more than anything. She had
smoked too much. And she got her pussy ate, and her
booty licked. *Butt cheeks all in his face.* A few more
minutes, and she was gonna ride that dick like a stallion.
What was a calmness was now a panic.

"Mes'siyah is on his way!"

"How do you know?"

"I know him!"

That's all Penelope needed to hear. She pushed them
niggas out, without even having Mar searched.

CHAPTER EIGHTEEN

North Philly...

"You sure he's in there?" Sacari asked.

They guy with the raspy voice he was talking to had come across some valuable information. And he wanted to be paid handsomely. When you rolled with Mes'siyah, your arms were long, and the reach had very few limits. Straight like that.

They were in a bar-and-grill, some seedy spot with excellent wings and slamming fries. The guy wiped his hands on a clean napkin, then wrote something down on another. Sacari read it, then said, *"Doable..."*

He handed Whispers 300 crispy c-notes.

Whispers finished his food, and Sacari rolled out. He was a one man show, Teflon vest on, two pistols by the waist. It took him twenty minutes to do the deed, and two minutes to make it back to the freeway. As he was pulling up on 57th Street, Nico was coming out of Lil Mama's crib. Sacari hit the horn, and Nico trotted over and hopped in.

"What's up, Bro?"

"He charged me thirty bandz for the info on mommy's dope dealer-slash-lover. So, I'm gonna need fifteen from you," Sacari said, his eyes glaring out he windshield of the black M5 Beemer.

"Why didn't you take me???" Nico asked, punching his left hand with his right one. "You see what I did on Croosky!"

"I'm gonna take you with me to handle something else, in due time…"

$ $ $

Villanova, PA…

By the time Mes'siyah got to the mansion, Rubi was gone. Watts tried to stop Mes'siyah and inform him of the visitors, but Mes'siyah waved him off and kept it pushing.

I'll slap those big dumb ass earrings out your ears young boy!, Sergeant Watts was thinking while shooting daggers into Mes'siyah with his eyes. *You've become a straight ass hole.*

Mes'siyah just had a lot on his mind. Like getting rid of Nico before Colombo and Carpenter connected him to the Croosky murders. Getting rid of Lil Mama before she started pillowing talking and Nico connected him to his mother's overdose. And then there was his cutthroat cousin, *Mally Gz*. And on top of that, his father wanted his take sent to him every week, as if he didn't already have enough money.

Mes'siyah wasn't thinking about Watts. And he seen the sergeant's nostrils flaring.

He shot up to Rubi's room first, and the door was locked. He started to kick it off the hinges. But he refrained. And Penelope kind of restrained him.

She had managed to also put his room back in tact before he reached there. "Your sister called me a concubine..."

"What should she had called you? A paramour?"

"She should have called me *your bitch*...."

"Clearly..." he said, cracking no smiles. "Where is that bitch?"

Penelope's eyebrows raised, and she folded her arms. She felt like Rubi didn't deserve that. She felt like no woman should be called a bitch unless it was being done tastefully. And although Rubi was changing right before Penelope's eyes, she still saw Rubi as the innocent little girl who once stuffed her bras with tissue. And now she was a young lady, doing her own thing. And it felt like Mes'siyah just couldn't take that.

Mes'siyah said, "Okay, she's not a bitch. But clearly she is getting on my last nerve. And I will not hesitate to send her to Baldwin Hills."

Penelope began to pout, push her plump lips forward, displaying further disappointment in her lover's lack of compassion and empathy for his younger sibling.

"You know where she is, don't you? She could be in danger, ma," he said to Penelope, circling her in a slow but deliberate gait.

Penelope spun in a small circle, maintaining her eye contact with him. 'She is fine…"

"And you know this how?"

Penelope was certain he didn't know Rubi had a man in the mansion. "Because I was with her."

With that, all movement stopped, and they were now face to face. Actually, lip to lip. "Are you fine, mister? You have bags under your eyes, and you are looking skinny too. *Flacito*…gosh…"

"What did you just call me?" he asked, his nicotine breath assaulting Penelope's nostrils.

"*Flacito*," she repeated. "It means—thin, skinny."

"I like Mes'siyah. It's more befitting of a king. Stick with that, you heard?"

"Clearly," Penelope said, now twirling a tress of her dark and lustrous hair around her right index finger. "Did you figure out what you're gonna do with your young boy Nico?"

"You feel like hanging out with me for a minute?"

"Clearly! I always wanna spend time with you. Duh! I am in love with you, man."

Penelope wanted to cuddle and just talk, canoodle a little bit, just be in his presence. But he had other plans.

"Take ya clothes off soon as you get up to my room."

Penelope grinned, showing a dimple, and said, *"Everything?"*

Mes'siyah nodded, then smacked Penelope on her juicy ass. And it shook nicely in her loose fitting gray Nautica sweatpants.

As she took to the stairs, he went through his social media. He noticed that an **R.I.P.** captioned on a pic of Trap God and his man Doc was trending. That meant, the kid Nico had shot had checked out. On another picture of Trap God and Doc, obviously taken when they were young teens, it said:

We will miss you, #Kinsington Royalty

Beneath it, Mes'siyah tagged:

Clearly! #UrbanRoyalty

Mes'siyah's ignorance was otherworldly. The kid had no conscience.

THE NEXT DAY, Mes'siyah boarded a private jet out to Cali, where he met up with Bish and voiced his concerns. No one could tell him that Mally Gz hadn't positioned himself on some underhanded shit. And he never imagined that Bish had actually made the decision for Mally Gz.

Mes'siyah would never outwardly admit it, but be looked up to and still admired his cousin from the Empire State.

When Mes'siyah was on the sideline watching as the brand was being built, Mally Gz was already in the thick of it. And he knew Mally Gz had worked overtime for everything that he acquired. His name, his worth, his spot—no stimulus packages! So it fulfilled Mes'siyah for Mally Gz to be answering to him. Calling him for the reup. It added pedigree to Mes'siyah's position in the streets. But the other way around, him reporting to Mally Gz, just wasn't sitting right.

He needed answers, and the roles immediately reversed back to the way they were.

The house in Baldwin Hills was immaculate. It didn't have the gates around it like the Villanova mansion. There was no long dazzling driveway, no artsy sculptures and structures to personify royalty, no armed guards. But, the infinity pool was bigger, the helipad was nicer, the front lawn seemed to go on forever. Then Mes'siyah liked the ginormous hip-roof with the magnificent windows. And the weather was amazing.

Bish was happy to see a familiar face. And it showed in his stride and the smile on his face.

Mes'siyah's face was stoic, and he was taking his time, each step slow and deliberate. He was tugging along two large military style duffels too.

Once Angel had settled into her last trimester, there was a plan in place for him to head back north. He missed Avery Trap. And seeing her blowing up on the internet, and the phone calls and video chats weren't cutting it.

"Young boy."

"Old head…"

"It's good to see you," Bish said, arms outstretched for the bags Mes'siyah quickly released.

"My mother inside?"

"She is…"

Mes'siyah went up the cobblestone walkway, and leaving his father behind, he stepped through the massive doorway.

"Momma!" he shouted, looking around. He could immediately tell she had all the influence on the decorum. *And Bish had no say so.*

My super control-ling mother, he thought as she emerged looking super pregnant.

"My baby!" she boomed. "You are here…"

They embraced, mother and son, while Bish watched them and fingered the now unzipped duffels at the same time. It wasn't just his take for being boss, it was all the money from the vault back in Villanova too. *Cold hard cash! And, eight million of it.*

"So, how are things back in Philly?" Angel asked, walking her boy by the hand to the modern and sensational kitchen. Everything was stainless steel except the redwood cabinets.

She made his favorite sandwich with all organic foods, made herself a smoothie, then they sat.

"You look malnourished and sleep deprived…"

"Penelope said the same thing."

"She watching you like that?" Angel snarled.

"Clearly mom."

"How are things with you and Ivory Manning? Keep

her close, you might need that card in ya pocket. And she really likes you for you, not your namesake."

"Allegedly," Mes'siyah said, chomping down.

"How is my daughter? I see her all over the *gram*, she's blowing up, and stepping into her own."

"She's smarter than I thought."

Angel said, "Smarter than I was at her age."

"Did you really catch her getting busy in a Hellcat?"

"Well, not really, but something sexual went down."

"Was it Trap Demigod?"

"Why you call him that?" Angel said, brows raised.

"Because I'm the trap god."

"I like that guy, that's why I invited him to her nineteenth birthday."

"Not because you think he might've busted in her in the Hellcat?"

"Mes'siyah!" Angel whined, smacking him on his arm. "That's my daughter. I can speak unkindly about her, you cannot. At least not to me."

"Clearly. You let her outsmart you, didn't you? Now she got Avery Trap looking like something."

"If Avery Trap hadn't been nearly killed by Smally G, she would still be a little known singer, on the King Music Group. She's still my artist. I discovered her. She's just being managed by my daughter. And a young sensation, still on King Music Group."

"Win win," Mes'siyah began, "I guess..."

With a not so hearty laugh, Angel said, "Clearly."

"I thought she outsmarted you. You're usually on top of things. You're getting old."

"I'll be forty this year coming. If you think that's old, then I'm old."

"Too old to be having another fucking baby."

"Were you allowed to cuss at me in any of my houses? Ah—*no*! Nothing's changed."

Mes'siyah didn't say anything.

"That Colombo and Carpenter still sniffing around?"

"Not that I know of."

"I heard you let Smally G's brother escape the kidnapping. And, several days later Sacari's mother overdosed?" Angel said, then sipped from her green smoothie. "Treacherous game we're playing. I never saw this happening when I gave you the location on Mar. I'm getting old, but you're acting like you don't want to get old."

Bish was spying on them. He always had. Just like he and Rubi were tight, Angel and Mes'siyah had a special bond. And the things he heard them saying just turned his stomach. Especially the stuff about his daughter.

"I sent the ransom demands, turned my back for a minute, and Mar was on the move, momma. I actually saw the fucka, naked and afraid, hop in Ms. Kourtney's car and haul ass."

"And right before that, Smally G is walking all over your car, and shooing at the gang," Angel said, shaking her head. The worse thing that had ever happened to them when they were Mes'siyah's age was when Smally G had gotten robbed and stripped naked. And the same way she and Bish had gassed Smally G up to

159

react, bring the pain, she was history repeating itself.

Clearly, Angel was disappointed. Her bright son, the force leading their movement now, and he was making mistakes like that. She knew he was in danger. She knew they were in danger. That's how the game went. No matter that he wasn't hands on. But what Angel didn't know was, Bish saw all this coming. He knew his son was more into fashion than he was into taking care of business. *That's why he was King! Exactly why he was looking to the future. Because Bish believed that even in his forties, he still had a future.*

"How is the gang?" she asked.

"We tight," Mes'siyah lied.

"Even after a hostage is released by Sacari's mom, and then she ends up dead? Watch ya self, boy."

"What you mean?"

"Smally G was once your dad's best friend. And like Nas said, *a thug changes, and love changes, and best friends become strangers.*"

"Nas is old, just like you," Mes'siyah said, shaking his head in disgust. Not with his mother, but with himself. With his current dilemma.

"You can get old, just don't get played out."

"Listen, I gotta get going, mom."

Without being excused, Mes'siayh left the kitchen, and located his father. "What's up pops?"

"We in an election year, things are hot, and—"

"I'm talking about me and you?"

"You are my son. We good."

"Then, why are we doing things different than what

we established six months ago?"

"We're in an election year. We're gonna either have the first female president or the first reality TV star for a president," Bish said, looking his son in the eye.

"Ah, what are you talking about?"

Bish said, "We are living in extraordinary times. That's what I am saying."

Mes'siyah's face fell into his hands, and he let out a sickening laughter. One of sheer frustration. "Yooo!"

"What?"

"I'm getting a hotel. I can't stay here."

Bish said, "Why not?"

"You cheating—"

"Cheating?"

"—on my mother with Avery Trap."

"Where that come from?" Bish asked, getting all up in Mes'siyah's face.

"You called me from her phone."

"You sure about that?"

Mes'siyah inhaled, then let it out, with "You take my position, and now you're talking to me like you're a fucking politician."

"Hang around them long enough you begin to adopt some of their politically correct answers, and you begin to understand preservation."

"Fix this before I head back north."

"Fix what?"

"The way things are—"

Bish cut Mes'siyah off. "The operation is gonna run through N.Y."

"So, I'm a do my own thing. Fuck yall."

"This is the second time you said some super fly shit to me. And I'm gonna address it the same way I did last time—*what the fuck you say, lil nigga???*"

Mes'siyah was caught off guard. Bish added some force to those words. He had grabbed Mes'siyah by the esophagus, tightened the grasp while looking his son in the eyes. It looked like the spirit was leaving Mes'siyah. So Bish let him go.

Mes'siyah caught his breath, then said, "You heard what I said. I done killed thirteen people. Don't start trying to be daddy now..." He then stormed out.

Angel only watched from the lounge window as Mes'siyah bopped off. Her smoothie was finished, but she knew the family feud was just beginning.

As Bish made his way back through the foyer, she was there to meet him.

Make no mistake, Angel was still a very gorgeous and vivacious woman. And she was glowing from the pregnancy. All of her body parts were plump and beautified. Her hair looked like it belonged to a Rican mami, her eyes were slanted like the Asians but with bright orbs, and her complexion was honey gold. But 39 years of age was no spring chicken. Especially with the boom of self-promotion all over the internet. Physically fascinating women from almost every corner of the world, advertising their sumptuous flesh. Some with enhancements, some photo-shopped, but all unquestionalbly unavoidable for an unhappy man. And the bossy, manipulative mannerisms in which Angel operated, diminished some of her appeal and attractiveness in the eyes of Bish.

He never got to know the earnest and naive Angel Ross. He didn't know she lost her virginity on a rooftop at 13- years of age. Or that she actually thought love was correlated with sex-consensual or nonconsensual. You fuck a guy, you belong to him now, or until he goes to prison or gets killed, she once thought. Bish didn't know she spent a lot of her time in recording studios, only to see her rhymes get someone else a record deal.

Bish met Angel when she had already realized the world was an unkind place, and good guys get got. By the she determined to be the designer of her destiny. And self -preservation is the first law of nature.

So, it should have been no surprise to Bish when Angel told him, "I am falling in love with you. "

The smart man he is today would have questioned her motives, been suspicious of her confessed affection for him so fast. They'd only know each other for a few weeks. But, that's how good she was. She could convince a 22-year-old Bish that he could rule the world with her by his side.

"...but we will never be safe with Smally around..." she had told Bish as they rode the   Amtrak down to Philly from New York. He had thoughts of killing his friend. But at the time Bish wasn't built like that. So, he came up with another plan. He put some stickup kid.

Then he pressed Smally G to retaliate.

But right before that, Angel had also told Bish that Smally G could possibly be the father of their first child, knowing that was the farthest thing from the truth. A ploy to further ignite rancor in Bish towards Smally G. When in fact Smally G had been dating her first.

As soon as Mes'siyah was born, the paternity was undisputed. Bishop King was the father. Then came the marriage.

Angel thought it was solely based on their chemistry in the bedroom and on the streets, coupled with the arrival of their Mes'siyah King. But Bish really did it official because when things backfired on them, and he ended up on State Road with no bail, Angel went hard to see him set free.

They had a dream and a promise of family and power. And through it all, they achieved that.

Angel didn't really want to keep Rubi when she found out she was pregnant with her second child. Angel wanted to step back in the booth, play the music scene. But Bish demanded she abort the thought of abortion. Then took her to Fiji for two weeks. There, in what felt like paradise he convinced Angel that after their first million dollars they could start their own recording label. That's why Rubi meant so much to him, and could do no wrong in his eyes.

Angel was just as along in that pregnancy as she was

in this one, her third…

As soon as Bish saw Angel standing there, the version of her who would be forty soon, pigeon-toed, belly poking out, he said, " 'Siyah staying in a hotel tonight, then heading back to Philly. I'm gonna sit down and run everything through the money machines. But by the eye test, it's all there… "

She noticed Bish didn't really give her his eyes. Just a quick meaningless glance. He was about to trot up the winding stairs, when he heard, "Is it still loyalty above royalty?"

"Loyalty over royalty, always. I love my family. That's why I'm going back to Philly…"

Angel rolled her eyes, and said, "I'm supposed to do what?"

"Brook Burnside, your best friend, spend some time with her. Finish telling her how you run this shit over here…"

Angel felt a pang in her heart. No matter how much shit she talked, no matter how bossy she could be, Angel had never done anything to push Bish away. At least, in her eyes. But, if distance plus time could equal space, the two of them were miles apart with the birth of their third child so close.

Angel sighed, puppy dog eyes on full display, and Bish still went in the opposite direction.

By 1 AM that morning, Bish was done stashing all

the loot, $9,080,000 of it, and a sexy young songstress was calling.

He perked up like he had a hot shot of Starbucks. And felt special. "You got a hit single booming on iTunes, and another song climbing the charts, and you were checking for me, forty-four-year-old Bish King, at this time of night?"

The call immediately turned to Facetime. And Avery Trap was in her midtown apartment, naked, saying "Yes. Sexy ass forty-four-year-old Bishop King." All giddy and shit.

"What are you doing up so late?" he asked, too smiling.

"I like talking to you in the middle of the night. I have your undivided attention, sir."

Bish could see the skyline of Manhattan out the window behind her. Even without the Towers, it was still a beautiful site to see. But   Avery   Trap   looked better. The contour of her breasts, the color of her deep brown areolas, the size of her thick nipples.

"I'm traveling north in the morning."

"I'm going to Atlanta in a few days."

"For?"

"Your daughter invited me to the BET Hip Hop Awards with her and the guy who did my first major video."

"Nice..." Bish said, nodding and stroking his beard.

"I may have to fly down to Atlanta."

" I think you should skip Philly and come straight to New York," Avery Trap shot back, laying on her back, her legs up like she was in some yoga position. "That is days away, Bishop. And, quite frankly, I miss your ass now."

"I miss you too, young lady."

"You are just so kind, so gentle, polite, and attentive, and gallant, and humble too. The world would be a better place if more men were like you."

Bish just chuckled, his way of saying he knows.

"Rubi has me booked up with shows all the way up until New Years Eve. I told her I will not perform in Philly again though. Never."

"Fear is only fear when it controls you," Bish said, shying away a bit.

Avery Trap said, "Didn't I tell you that???"

The two shared a cozy laughter, that was brief but nice, then Avery Trap said, "I would be able to point him out if I ever saw him again."

Bish already and always knew who the shooter was, so he felt somewhat disingenuous, almost forgetting he is a street dude. And a gangster in the eyes of many. And that even though he knew Smally G, her being shot wasn't on him.

While watching Bish, her phone close to her face, Avery Trap said, "I would still be average, leading a mundane life, and questioning my entire existence had I not been shot. Which brings me to this…"

"What?"

"I am indebted to Rubi for taking my drip to the next level. She got ya girl getting tweets from RiRi and the Queen B!"

"You were already validated, doing something you love, and invested time and money in. Things happen when they're supposed to, not when we want them to."

"So, everything you've accomplished happened when it was supposed to? Is that what you're telling me? You never sped up the process? You never skipped the line? You never enforced your will? Because I know different. The Bishop King I know of is a taker."

"What are you saying?"

"I want production on my full-length record to begin soon. I want to be a priority on King Music Group. I want a big budget so I can work with some of the top producers. I want you in New York more often too, so we can spend more time together."

"What type of budget are we talking?"

Avery Trap was thinking big. She saw her rood rise. Possibility was now riding behind. Avery Trap said, "One million!"

"The business isn't the same--"

"Yeah, but here's the deal. You can say no, and let me out my recording contract. Our plans to be a unit will still move forward, I just won't be recording--"

"You have some incredible breasts. Perfect d-cups," Bish told her, licking his lips. "And this isn't how business deals are made. Naked beauties and execs--"

"You're right. My bad."

"No problem."

"Can I show you something else?" she asked.

"Yes, you can."

Avery Trap pointed the camera on her iPhone at her clean shaven and puffy pussy lips...

BOOG DENIRO

CHAPTER NINETEEN

October, 2016 …

The weather had hit a switch on the east coast. It was time for leather jackets. Bish was wearing one from the fall line of his clothing company. And he had on a black 76ers cap with the brim pulled low over his aviator shades. He had just come from a barbershop in West Philly, not far from Hoop Street. Whispers met him there. Bish got a tight line on his Caesar cut and his fluffy beard, while Whispers had everything shaved off making him resemble a Black Mr. Clean.

As they were leaving, Whispers said, "I don't know how you did it, but you did it."

"My nephew convinced me that he owned powerful thoughts. And everything starts in the mind. Every single thing. If you can imagine it, you can put it into existence. He imagined us rebuilding our organization. And I agreed."

"I'm not talking about that. I'm talking about clearing

the path for the beginning of your new life."

Bish took the aviators off, squinted from the strong and bright rays. He said, "Excuse me?"

"You shipped the wife off to the west coast. And now you can play a little bit."

"I ask to meet so we could discuss business, not my personal life."

"Right, right," Whispers replied with the cotton mouth and utter disbelief. He thought he could overstep that boundary, being as though he knew so much.

"I thought he would flee the city, and the fucking state, when he found his mother dead ..."

"Ice cold," Whispers said, smiling again.

"But he come on strong, and I don't know where he is. It's bothering me."

"That coke you got coming in, from the Mountain Brothers, I need parts." Whispers didn't wait for a response. "I handled something for your son, and I was compensated with couple a block of that shit. And, quite frankly, I ain't seen nothing like it since the early nineties."

Bish returned the aviator shades back to the bridge of his nose, walked to the right back door of the Rolls Royce where two armed men awaited his return. "Well, good for you."

"His main man Sacari, he's been seeking my advice a little bit lately too."

"He's a fucking kid, Whispers."

"He's a fucking killer, and a grieving one."

"Sound like you're talking about Smally G. A grieving killer."

"In that case, I understand your problem," Whispers said, looking up one end of the block and then down to the other end.

The conversation was getting weird, and they both knew it. But neither really knew why, other than, things that once mattered to them no longer held the same significance. For one, Whis pers felt like he should've been running things, and not the New York nephew, while Bish never really saw Whis pers as anything other than a henchman.

But what Bish didn't know was that Mes'siyah had confided in Whispers about his resentment towards his father, while hiring him to off his right-hand man's mother. Whispers was so vicious, he sent Sacari to kill someone else he had taken money to put on a first class trip straight to heaven. Yeah, Whispers was playing like he had the best hand. He was betting on himself.

"I'll see what I can find out, but I want five of them bricks for this one."

"What did my son give you two for?"

"You're gonna have to ask him that."

Bish was shocked. "Really???"

"Yeah. Confidentiality. By the way, that black leather

jacket you're wearing is mean, brother. Think you can throw one of them in?"

"What size?"

"Extra-large?" With that, Whis pers slid into his white $550.

AN HOUR LATER, Bish pulled up to the gates of the Villanova mansion. As soon as they were the black Rolls Royce, the gates opened. As soon as the driver parked, Bish got out and looked around. He was home, and it felt good. Rubi's new car was there, and so was Mes'siyah's...brand new all white Wraith.

Bish walked into his home, bumping right into Penelope whom happened to be startled by her boss's presence.

"Mr. King?" she said.

"Penelope, it's good to see you." He noticed a glow about her, and that she wasn't wearing her uniform. "Don't let anyone know I'm here."

As soon as Bish said that, Watts came in, having slowed his trot. "It's good to see you, sir. No erratic driving was there? I was sleep-"

"Good to see you too. What's been going on?"

"Things have been weird around here lately.

" Bish said, "On what tip???"

"My job is security. So, I've noticed a lot of traffic lately. And the staff has been dressed down. Your daughter is dating Mes'siyah has been digressing. And, there is no leadership. Everyone seems to be doing their own thing these days, sir."

Penelope was just around the corner listening, and could not wait to tell Mes'siyah what she had just heard.

"Thank you, Mr. Watts. Just keep doing what you're being paid to do," Bish said before moving along.

Bish walked down the corridor, didn't stop forward progress until he was in is version of the oval office. Right where he wanted There were framed pictures of past civil rights leaders, autographed photos of modern-day sports icons, and a life-size portrait of his long dead mother. Bish didn't know his father, and had no knowledge of grandparents. That's why it was so easy for him to buy into Angel's vision of family when she promoted it in the 90's. Everything was just the way he'd left it. Except the vault was now empty, with the door slightly ajar. He sat on his throne like chair, the burgundy Italian leathered upholstery squeaking like it was still very fresh.

The BET Hip Hop Awards were just 36 hours away, and Rubi was beyond excited. She's been posting vlogs about her ensuing trip, as well as tweeting all morning. It was the biggest event she'd ever been invited to. And the Kings attended all kinds of' functions over the years.

Just the night before, Rubi had smoked her magical blunt, then got Avery Trap on the phone. The synthetic drug had the ability to hinder, alter or energize Rubi's thoughts. Depending on how, many puffs she settled on. Within minutes, and with a cool and mellow approach, she had convinced the singer to come to Philly.

Rubi knew her father had taken the helicopter to Cali, but still said, "I'm sending my dad's chopper. It'll land on your roof, pick you up, and bring you straight here where you'll be safe, take us to the airport where we will meet Young Godd and his entourage."

Instead of Bish's chopper landing on Avery Trap's Manhattan rooftop, a local helicopter pilot was paid to scoop her up.

Bish's eyes nearly popped out of his head when he saw an unidentified chopper landing on his heliport, her black and gray Gucci luggage the rear entrance.

He watched on the monitor as Rubi and Avery Trap embraced in pure jubilation. He then clicked on the monitor that allowed him to peek in on his son. Mes'siyah was holding Penelope in his arms, looking right into the camera. He knew his father, and he knew all about his pop's bird's eye view.

Bish exited the footage of Mes'siyah's bedroom, hit rewind on the hard-drive covering footage of the last two weeks. He could've gone back even further, but he just wanted a quick glimpse into the unhappy land he hadn't created. Bish had worked overtime to give his family the best of everything.

All the monitors were now lit!

Avery Trap eyes moved fast and uncontrollable. There was so much to take in. She knew the Kings were Urban Royalty, but the art, the sculptures, the furnishings, the white china, the illustrious decorum spoke volumes. Pure opulence!

Something like this could be mine, Avery Trap reasoned with a grin when she was taken by surprise.

Rubi was high as fuck, and busy scrolling through the flowing and glowing comments on her social media pages. The love she wanted from her family, she believed she was getting from social media, not realizing affirmation and adoration there could just as quickly flip to ridicule and judgment by people she could very well never ever meet.

By the time she turned around, with this winning smile on her face, Avery Trap had just vanished into thin air. But her luggage remained.

Rubi's took a brief gander, looking around, then her normally bright eyes, now low and·hazy, went right back to her phone screen. She swiped and read while her feet took her towards the kitchen area. She had the munchies.

As quick as the secret door slipped open, Bish slid it back into its inconspicuous place, and Avery Trap was a few steps behind Bish inside walls of the mansion, traveling back to the oval office. "Bishop …" she cooed, feeling the warmth of his hand on her wrist, as he led the way.

"Hey, sugar ..." he replied as they came to the brightness of the 100-watt bulbs lighting the office. "What are you doing in Philadelphia? I mean, I'm happy to see you, though surprised since you said you were against returning."

"Duhhh, I wanted to see you. And I knew you'd be home from the west coast ..."

"Can I kiss you?"

Avery Trap said, "You can do whatever--"

Bish slipped his tongue in her mouth, and she could taste the Big Red gum on it. Sparks were flying.

"I see where you get your handsome features from, Bishop," Avery Trap said, when her eyes popped back open.

The photo of his mother was taken in 1967, nearly forty years ago. She put you in the mind of the female revolutionary Angela Davis with the big afro and gorgeous features. If Bish mother were alive, she would've been 68-years old.

"Thank you," Bish said, before going in for another kiss. His lips covered hers, his tongue caressed hers his hands roamed her shapely and nimble body. He then kissed her neck, her collarbone, her cleavage which was exposed by the plunging neckline on her swanky top. While he hungrily nibbled on her, she looked around biting her bottom lip. She saw the monitors, the vaults, the huge desk, the money machines. She thought the cemetery resembled the Oval Office at 1600 Pennsylvania Avenue.

Bish was already her dream guy, but now he was kissing all over her in his mansion, in a secret room only seen in films. She could not believe it. She was blown away, and felt like she was in a movie.

"Wait, wait, wait, my guy," she said, taking her straight to his Gucci belt buckle. "I want your dick in my mouth."

While she was trying to free his erection in his jeans, Bish's eyes were drawn to one of the monitors. He watched intently, saw Rubi throwing up like the girl in the scene from the Exorcist movie. Rubi then stripped out of her clothing, which wasn't much, just a thong and a tank top, and began swimming in the shallow pool of vomit.

Rubi's floors were   marble, and pink and white tiled because she loved Nicki Minaj so much.

Penelope was on camera discovering Rubi that way, and Bish was watching as his maid cared with concern for his only begotten daughter.

For him, it was beyond bizarre, but more importantly something Avery Trap could never see.

Rubi went from the breast stroke, to the back stroke, completing each and every movement as if the rancor mess was actually water. While on her back, Rubi rubbed the food that had to have disagreed with her stomach all over her pretty face. Laughing all the while…

It was at that moment that Avery Trap felt Bish's lips on her again, then his hand on the small of her back, rushing her back through the secret tunnel in the wall of the mansion.

"Wassup, Bishop? Did I do something wrong?" Her feet weren't moving as fast as his. "Wait, hun!"

As the secret door was sliding back shut, Bish said, "I will call you in a few minutes."

"Oh, there you are!!!" Rubi said, eating a Milkshake Pop Tart she toasted.

Glancing back at the wall, looking for a groove, any sign of the secret door, Avery Trap said, "Here I am…"

In less than a minute, Bish was back at the desk watching intently. He hit the rewind button. Stopped where he seen Rubi rolling in her own vomit like a mentally ill person.

Bish found some other footage, saw Rubi rolling a blunt. In was a different day, and she was wearing something different as well. She hit the blunt, once, twice, three times, then a fourth. He noticed her begin to panic, hyperventilate, then strip out of her clothes. Ber lips were moving, so he turned the volume up. Rubi was saying, " I'm hot. They hot. My tit! Cut them off. Cut my titties off …" She grabbed an Apple Mac Pro laptop and began fanning her chest area. "Water, I need water …!" She tilted the laptop upward, angling it over her tits.

It became clear to Bish that his daughter was hallucinating, and smoking an hallucinate. It was the new wave. No, more like an epidemic in urban communities, and the prisons across the nation.

Bish watched more. In some of the footage, Rubi took one or two pulls, and seemed to be in deep thought. She was posting, taking selfies, dancing and singing in Snapchat videos. In others, she appeared to be secluded, reclusive, paranoid, or just out of her mind, just trying to come back to reality.

"...where you at daddy? Are you under there? I just saw you go under the bed. If you come out, I won't ask Avery Trap if she is fucking my dad... "

Rubi had gone underneath her California king bed, looking for her father, and nearly five minutes had passed before she crawled back out howling like a wolf.

And in another recorded episode, Rubi had smoked until she collapsed, and appeared to have been paralyzed from the neck down. Her words were slurred, and she was saying, "How come my mother and my brother hates me???"

Bish felt bad, and far removed from judgment. He had experimented with drugs in the past. He just wanted to console Rubi, and get her some help before she went into one of those mental breakdowns and never returned. And then...he saw Charleston Smallwood. Alone with his Rubi, in her room, holding a blunt up to her lips, whispering,"…hit it again, again, again, and again. Hold it in…"

Rubi was smiling, naked, and so was Charleston Smallwood·.

"No, this nigga didn't! He's fucking my precious daughter???

And done turned her out on K2???. "

CHAPTER TWENTY

Baldwin Hills, CA...

"Brook, I'm beginning to feel like Tasha. " Angel told her best friend, while sitting out back poolside "

"Tasha who? And, why do you feel like her?"

"Power. Tasha, St. Patrick. The 50 Cent show..."

"Oh. Okay. Not a watcher of that show. Is Tasha pregnant???"

" No! Tasha is being cheated on!" Angel boomed.

Brook said, "You think Bish is having an affair?"

"Something is going on."

"Oh. Wow. That sucks," Brook bemoaned, then continued with, "That man worships the ground you walk on, girl."

Angel said, "Not anymore. He doesn't even look at me the same. I think I know who it is too."

"Whom is she???"

"That is not how you use...whom?"

"Well, who is she?"

Angel held her phone tightly, pursed her lips as the tears began to flow. "The Realtor. That fucking bitch Thaila."

"What does it matter, anyway?"

"She conveniently finds us this home. She spent nearly two day with Bish. And what do you mean, what does it matter??? That's my man, my husband, I'm carrying his child, I gave him two other children! Fuck!"

"What I mean is, you want for nothing. You have everything.

Women would give a kidney to be in your stilettos, girlfriend."

Angel, huffed and puffed, then said, "I would have given him a kidney."

"Trust me, I know…"

"I put into the success as much as he did, Brook. And, you know I did! Ground up type shit! He had three thousand dollars when we met. He was driving a Honda Accord station."

"Facts. But Honda wagon was the shit when you two met."

"It wasn't a Rolls Royce."

"Facts."

"And I don't deserve this. Know what I'm saying, Brook?"

"Angel, I also know that you can exaggerate things, "Brook said, as she straightened up some things on her desk that seemed to be out of place.

"Like what???"

"Like, that day last summer, at the block party. You didn't know whether or not Rubi was having sex in that car. Yet, you did not hesitate to put the jumper cables on that. I was just thinking: that is not true. You didn't catch her doing anything.

And I just thought that wasn't cool. It wasn't my place to say anything though."

Angel didn't respond.

"Can I tell you something else?" Brook asked while looking at her fresh white manicure.

Angel said, "Go ahead."

"I looked up to, a real boss bitch from the Bronx. In fashion, winning in music, winning in your everyday life. Until that day... "

"Until what day???" Angel boomed.

"Last summer, the day Avery Trap was shot. Your actions, your behavior, towards Rubi, someone you brought into this world, knocked you down several notches."

Angel hung up on Brook. That's how much the truth hurts. And she cried. For years she controlled everyone and everything in her orbit. Either through finesse, or with force. The method didn't matter, only that she got her way. Now her son was a killer, looking to break away from the family. Her daughter hated her, and was coming into her own. And her husband couldn't even look at her.

Angel wasn't the doting mother, and she wasn't the loving wife that she projected onto the masses. Angel was a bitch!

Her ringtone sounded off

Coffee, by Miguel.

She didn't answer it, thinking it was Brook calling her back. But actually, it was her husband and business partner.

$ $ $

Villanova, PA…

Bish was pacing uncontrollably. His sneakers were squeaking on the marble floor, and his back teeth were grinding…

One thing about success, it can be blinding. And that's exactly what happened with Smally G. He was experiencing some success. That's if you are of the school of thought that small victories lead to big ones.

He got the half million off Bish. What a starter kit that was! He shot up Mes'siyah's block party, putting two holes in Avery Trap's flesh. He walked on top of Mes'siyah's Bentley coupe, then shot at him and the gang. He had Rubi strung out on his loving, and drugs. And he now knew where Bish rested his head. Oh, and his brother had returned from a kidnapping without him paying the ransom.

To date, though tragic, Smally G had only lost his mother, a woman he had very few feelings for anyway.

Bish was deep in thought. He needed to vent. But Angel had sent all her calls to voice mail. He decided to take a hot shower, just let the steamy water run over his head.

When Bish exited the walk-in 15x20sq. foot shower, Avery Trap was standing there. She had managed to sneak off, and make her way into the steamy bathroom which was part of the master bedroom.

She locked both doors, the one she came through, and the one that led to the master bed, with Bish watching her every move.

"You can't get a sistah hot and bothered, then leave me hanging,"Avery Trap told him, while coming out of her Gucci slides, jeans and boy shorts. Now the only thing she was wearing was that swanky top with the plunging neckline. "I know you' re the man, but let me find out you getting boujee on a sistah, Bishop???"

"You the one acting boujee," Bish shot back, droplets of water still covering his lean but toned physique.

Something was different, and Avery Trap noticed it immediately. Facial expression, demeanor, cadence and candor, all different. Nothing really ever got by Avery Trap.

"What? How? "she said as gentle as possible, and now completely naked. Her breasts, full and bouncy, were calling Bish's name. Her pouty pussy lips were positioned right where the gap separated her thick thighs. And her booty was so juicy and plump, Bish could see it from the front. He wanted to reach out and touch her bullet wounds, let her know it would all work out. Then kiss all over her.

Avery Trap said, "What?"

"You get a million views on one video, six-digit streams, and you're making demands now???" he questioned, while drying his big balls and his dick with this fluffy teal blue towel.

There were mirrors everywhere in this bathroom, wall to wall and Bish liked performing in front of them. "You think a million views, and some streams equates to a million bucks?"

With supreme confidence, and the sassiness of a diva, yet sure to not spoil the moment, Avery Trap said, "I think I deserve more. Big facts. And, I know my worth."

Bish slid the glass doors back open, reached back into the shower and turned the dual shower heads back on. As it steamed back up, he said, "Get in. I haven't fucked in a shower since I was in a young man ..."

All the anger, and that justifiable fury Bish was harboring was unleashed on Avery Trap. Her 28-year-old body released three orgasms by the time he was finished pounding her tight and slippery pussy cat.

BEFORE THE SUNSET, Mally Gz was pulling up at that front gates of the mansion. He wasn't with the shot-'em-up bang-bang shit, but his man from High Bridge certainly was.

Mally Gz didn't know exactly what was going on, only that Uncle Bish wanted some work put in.

When Mes'siyah saw his cousin, Mally Gz, in the front room, standing all militant, with the stranger dude by his side, he said, "There was a time I was popping up on you for the gwap. Now you popping up on me???"

"I'm here to see uncle Bish. You got until Halloween to get with me, bee."

Penelope was close to Mes'siyah's hip, and Mally Gz had to admit, she was a joint. A baddie. Whatever you want to call an incredibly beautiful woman.

Penelope felt like Mally Gz was undressing her with his eyes. And, she didn't like the way the words came out of Mally Gz's mouth when he spoke to her lover. She rolled her eyes at him.

In all black denim, his leather jacket under his arm, Bish descended the winding stairs with a scowl on his face. He felt a bit better, because the sex was amazing, and Avery Trap had even given her secret lover a marvelous dick suck. But he was still under the mindset that his family was out of control and on the brink of self-destruction.

"Son,bee, kid, dog, you in my motherfucking house. Show some respect," Mes'siyah said, then gave his cousin dap. He whispered in Mally Gz' s ear, "I see the way you looking at my bae man."

Mally Gz didn't find any humor in Mes'siyah's quip, but still shook his hand.

"Anyone sees Avery! I can't find her, "Rubi said, her eyes bouncing from person to person.

"I'm right here, gurl!" Avery Trap sounded off, coming towards everyone as the breeze from chandelier hitting her wet flesh sent a chill up her spine.

Everyone was looking at Bish though, as his presence commanded attention. He was about to say something, make an announcement, when his phone buzzed. It was the address he'd been waiting for.

Bish kissed Rubi on her forehead, when he got to the crowd in his house, gave Mally Gz dap and a hug, then said, "I don't want anybody in my house who doesn't work here, or live here, as of today. I'm sure I made myself clear." He looked down at his daughter.

"No friends? Like, how am I gonna tell my friends they can't come see me? Come on, that makes no sense, daddy!"

He snatches Rubi so hard, everyone there could feel his power. Bish whispered "Especially you"

Rubi was daddy's little girl. Either Bish was having

a midlife crisis, or Philly was about to freeze over, came to Mes'siyah's mind. He locked eyes with his father. And with a faint roll of those eyes, he draped his arm over Penelope's shoulders and stepped off laughing. He knew that would piss his father·off. And to further fan the fire, Mes'siyah said, "Clearly. Yo, pardon my back …"

Rubi looped her arm through Avery Trap's arm, and they decided to skedaddle too, with Rubi's heart thumping.

Bish's breathing turned to heaving. He grabbed Rubi by the tricep, and seethingly said, "Smally is bad news..."

"Huh?" Rubi muttered, as Avery Trap gave them some space.

"Charlie…bad news, Rubi…"

Rubi's jaw dropped. She had only told Imani about her older boyfriend.

Bish had a picture of him in his phone; a picture of Smally G in a prison yard. He showed it to Rubi, said, "He's bad news. Don't ever see him again. Only the two of them could hear what he was saying.

Rubi knew her father was capable of everything. But spying on her??? She never had him under that act.

"Come on, we out, " Bish told Mally Gz and his comrade, leaving Rubi with her mouth ajar.

Twenty minutes later, Bish was in the Logan section of Philly with Mally Gz and the shooter. The autumn of chills had 19 degrees feeling like below zero, so there weren't many people outside. Without much attention being brought to them, Bish, Mally Gz and the triggerman entered the 2-story home through the back way.

At first Antonita didn't hear the rattling of the back door. Too busy on social media. Plus, she had never expected and intruder even though she had created some enemies of her own over the years. Because her enemies were behind bars, and walls, and I solitary confinement, instead of instinctively going for her firearm, Antonita with that fat butt shot to her son's bedroom first. And, unarmed. He was still sleeping, behind her with him in her arms. That's when she heard, "Correction officer Antonita Roman, right? And Smally G's prodigal son. Hey, young buck, you look just like my old chum..."

CHAPTER TWENTY-ONE

After the stunt he pulled, Mes'siyah was surprised Bish had called him with the newest location on Smally G. But in reality, Bish didn't do it for him, he did it to protect the King brand. Smally G had been on the move for too long, and poking the bear a bit too much.

Bish had said, "Go and take care of that, killer ..."

Mes'siyah wasted no time phoning Sacari. Only Sacari didn't pick up. So, Mes'siyah swung by Lil Mama 's crib where he found her with mascara and eye-liner blackening her tears. Before anything left Lil Mama's mouth, Mes'siyah lips were forming into a snare. He couldn't just be happy for his young boy, because he had sexed her first. He had possessive tendencies, and looked down on her. In his eyes, she was worthless. And incapable of feeling anything other than dicks. But, oh was he wrong.

"What you crying for?" he asked, standing in her living room where she sat on the floor, knees pulled tight

193

to her bust.

"They got Nico!"

"Who?"

"They came here and took him!" she blurted as she looked up with agony filling her eyes.

"Fuck is you talking about?"

"Homicide detectives. They came and picked him up, took him right out of my house. He's gone! My man is gone!"

"Wha--? Wait! Hold up…"

She pointed to a business card on her   c o f f e e table.

Detective Colombo, Homicide Division, Philadelphia PA…

Sacari hadn't answered Mes'siyah's call because he was on the phone with Nico. That's what he told Mes'siyah before saying, "They arrested him for the Doc murder."

"I told that nigga to go to fucking York!" Mes'siyah ranted, shaking his head.

And Lil Mama countered with, "Doc wasn't even dead yet when you suggested that…"

Mes'siyah muted his phone, then told Lil Mama, "Shut your fucking mouth. Fuck out of here."

"You in my house. You get the fuck out of here!"

"You know who the fuck I am??? Clearly! So, cut it out," he shot back with a snarl

Lil Mama's eyes got tight, and more tears flowed. He wasn't supposed to know she knew Doc was still alive, though in critical condition. Was the slip of her tongue. The only person she could be mad at was herself. At the same time, she was beginning to think Mes'siyah had inside information. She knew for a fact that dude wasn't dead when Mes'siyah was trying to send Nico out of town.

Mes'siyah un-muted the phone, said, "We got the drop on the small fry now. And, I need you"

Sacari said, "Where the fuck you at?"

"Lil Mama's crib…"

"Cool…" and the line went dead.

As Mes'siyah was heading for the door, Lil Mama jumped up and said, "Ain't you fucking the DA's daughter or some shit like that?"

"All I'm gonna say to you is, we gonna get the little nigga back out here on these streets. And don't you ever ask me who I'm fucking."

She grabbed Mes'siyah by his lanky arm, and said, "I dig the shit out that young nigga."

"Well, me and his brother been bros for thirteen years.

Which means, I knew Nico since he was four. He's like a little brother to me. Now relinquish my arm. I got places to be."

"Fuck you, Mes'siyah! I don't give two fucks if

195

you like me, or not. Before I decided I wanted to give Nico some pussy, and he starts staying here with me and my son, me and you were cool. Now, you on some nut shit!!"

"You older than me. So, you are too old for him," Mes'siyah began, staring her down, "And you been around. He with me; he supposed to be shacked up with a chick that ain't been around. Clearly."

"Old??? Ha! Picture that. Been around??? Tsst! Nigga, paaalease. You are so fucking extra. I sleep with who I like. My mind, my body, my decision. Don't try to pull that shit on me. If I wanted to, I could be really out there, leaching on rappers and ball players. And you know it. Look at this fucking face. Look at this body. Even my feet are delicious. Is you stupid???" She straight went off on Mes'siyah. "Every pic I post get two-hundred and fifty likes!"

"Listen, we gotta work together, like we did before."

"Before??? You got what you wanted, ttsss, and I didn't hear from you again. That's the way I recall it, Mes'siyah. You should just be called Extra Messy. You are so fucking messy, dude. And extra as fuck!"

Mes'siyah laughed.

It was a sad time for him, for his fa mily, and for his gang. But that was funny, and brave of Lil Mama to call him out on his defects and deficiencies.

And Lil Mama released a sigh of relief. She was sure

Mes'siyah was gonna act impulsively, and cause her further pain. The physical kind too.

She exhaled, and applauded herself for sticking up for herself. She was in this sexy ass black cat suit, hair, nails and toes done. She said, "I'm going to see Nico tomorrow. Should I tell him anything?"

Mes'siyah said, "Just don't tell him that you got his mother killed."

ON THE OTHER SIDE of Lil Mama's door and I the brisk night air, Mes'siyah dreaded the reality that he and Lil Mama were connected forever. Why??? Because she had life insurance. How??? Colombo and Carpenter knew exactly who Lydia "Lil Mama" Bell was…

And on the other side of that door, Lil Mama was flipping Mes'siyah the bird.

Sacari pulled up in front of Lil Mama's crib. Mes'siyah had Sacari follow him to the King Music Group recording studio, where he parked his car and retrieved a bag of tactical equipment from the trunk. Night vision goggles, 223's and 7.6 rounds.

Once inside, Mes'siyah told Sacari where they were headed, "Upper Darby, gang-gang."

Sacari just drove, traveling by side streets only. He didn't know what to say to Mes'siyah. His brother was on State Road, with grown ass men, and no bail. His mother was dead and gone. He just drove in silence, kind of erratic too. But, when Mes'siyah said, "We gonna get him out this…" whip-fast, Sacari replied, "You got him in the streets!"

"I got you in the streets too," Mes'siyah replied snidely, and watching Sacari drive like they weren't two deep with five guns with drums attached to them. "We gotta see what they got. Then go from there."

"I wanted to keep him out the streets. I wanted his to go away from Philly. Get an education."

"God had other plans."

"That's the problem, you really think you a God. And its part my fault, because I let you buy into the fairytale."

"You just mad right now," Mes'siyah said, looking ahead. "I can't lose my brother too."

"Clearly…" Mes'siyahs said, knowing all of this shit was on his hands. Like Lil Mama said, he was messy.

"That's my fucking brother. My only one!" Sacari wept, beginning to question everything. "I gotta ask you this? Where is sibling???" Sacari wanted to know. "Bet she ain't in jail."

At that very moment, Rubi was doing the un-thinkable.

"We gotta talk," Rubi was saying to Smally G.

Smally G was smoking a blunt of K2 with his brother Mar, while wiping down guns with a damp rag. "Rubi???" he said, as if he didn't recognize her voice.

"Duuuhhh,"she sounded off rolling her eyes. These days Smally G wanted her more than she wanted him.

"I miss you, Red Rubi, "he wasted no time telling her, while putting the call on speaker so Mar could hear him running his game.

"Charlie?"

"That's a fact. It's me baby. You miss daddy? Thought you was heading to the BET Awards?" he said. He planned to run up in the mansion while she was away in Atlanta, with his brother by his side, and lay everything down. But what he didn't know was his brother had sold the watch he stole out the mansion, and was planning on leaving town right before the planned attack.

"First of all, you are not my daddy. So, I don't know where that came from. But I suggest you ship it back first class."

"What?"

"You heard me. My dad's name is Bishop kind. You know my father too. And you forgot to tell me."

"I know a lot of people, "Smally G said, not liking the look on his brother's face, or the way this conversation was going.He took two pulls off his magical blunt.

"He has a fucking picture of you in his phone, when you were in prison! He knows you."

"Well, then, I know that. fool," he said, holding in the smoke he had inhaled.

"And you didn't think you should have told me you know my folks? Like, really??? Who the fuck does that?"

A bit dazed now, Smally G said, "Listen, you're

royalty. Everyone knows ya pops. I wasn't gonna be dick riding and shit, like a groupy. I'm a boss like he a boss, baby. "

Rubi was fuming.

"You there, Rubi???"

"I'm here. We got to break this off. I'm a need you to lose my number. Annnnd, I'm a lose yours..."

Smally heard that hesitation, and quickly hung up. He face-timed Rubi. They were now looking at each other when Smally G said, "I love you, Rubi King. I love ya lil ass."

"Wait, what?"

"I wanna meet up with your father. Set it up. I'd rather meet your father, smooth things out, and get his blessing, before letting you walk out my life..."

"You said you love me?"

"Since the first time I laid eyes on you. I'm your first. I took your virginity. You love me too. I'm the first nigga you ever gave that pussy too. The first nigga to stick his tongue in ya butt while he was eating that box ."

"I don't know that I love you, or that you love me, Charlie. Sex and loving someone should be separate. I think. we haven't even spent enough time together for all that. An hour or two here and there that is it."

"You don't love me??? Hold hold, you don't love Charlie???"

"Charlie stop.Stop it.You sounding all corny and shit.

And, I can't think straight right now."

He gave her this look that just turned her on. Then he licked his lips, put his blunt to his lips and took a tote.

He then said,"I wanna come over. Can I come over?"

" No! My brother and them is on their way to you! They are gonna kill you. You have to get out of there."

Smally G quickly hopped up, looking around. He was paranoid, but thinking he was on point. He went to the window,

the one that showed him the streets below and out front, then the one that showed the back alleyway. Smally G was high as fuck, thinking he was invincible.

Rubi called back, "You still there???"

"I'm leaving now. I'm on my way to you! I'm coming to get what's mine."

"I am not yours. You tripping."

"Where all this cocky shit come from?"

"You lying and scheming. That's where. And the only reason I called you was because-"

"I really love you."

Rubi sighed. This nigga was pussy whipped. And she kind of liked that. She said, "I'm not hanging up until you are out of there. And safe since you love me so much."

With Mar right behind him, the both of them holding heavy heat, Smally G headed for the back door.

Sacari was on the other side of the back door. The door was made of oak wood, and thick, but it splintered, nearly breaking in half, when Sacari pulled that trigger.

BANG! BANG! BANG! BANG! BANG!

BOCKA! BOCKA! BOCKA! BOCKA!

Behind Sacari was two of their other boys, who rushed to the address, eager to prove their worth to the unit.

"Go,go,go,go!"Smally G urged, back pedaling and ducking the onslaught.

BOCKA! BOCKA! BOCKA! BOCKA!

Smally G and Mar got low. They had made sure all the light were out already.

But the night vision goggles made Sacari and Mes'siyah advantageous. And they charged right in. There was no way Smally G and his little brother would make it out of there alive.

"Smalllllly," Mes'siyah called out, tauntingly. "Mar-Mar!

You got away once, but you won't again..."

Mes'siyah and Sacari were moving with meaning and passion, and towards the scurrying of feet of two high and nervous brothers.

Brrrraaaaatttt!

"Fuck!I just missed him!" Mes'siyah said, laughing and trotting towards the warm bodies.

A phone hit the floor. Brown carpet. The phone was face up. Mes'siyah leaned over, scooped it up, grinning.

"They're heading towards the back door!" Sacari warned, leaving Mes'siyah behind.

Mes'siayh put the phone in his pocket, as he caught up with Sacari and the other two shooters. They were running towards brisk air, and right into Smally G returning fire.

Pop, pop, pop, pop, pop, pop, pop!

Mes'siyah spueezed

Bbbbbrrrrrrrrrat!

Bbbbbrrrrrrrrrat!!

Smally G quickly realized they were at a huge disadvantage.

Semi autos versus automatic weaponry.

Nevertheless, Smally G wasn't shining them guns for a gun show. He planned on using them

Boom! Boom! Boom! BOOM! BOOM!

Mar followed suit- Pow! Pow! Pow!

"Oooh shit!" Sacari shrieked, pushing Mes'siyah back into the house. Smally G had tricked them. And it forced them back inside the house, giving Smally G enough time to board his getaway car.

Rubi could hear all the shots being fired, and cringed at each one. She was sure Smally G was as good as dead. She called out, "Charlie! Charlie! Say something, Charlie!"

Mes'siyah recognized his sister's voice.

Sacari was peeking out them doorway, and taking aim, paying Mes'siyah no mind.

Mes'siyah stuck his weapon out the door

Brrrrraatttt!

Brraaatttttttt!

He then turned his back to Sacari, pulled the phone from his pocket. Looking at the phone screen, he said to his little sister, "How the fuck ya little ass know this muthafucka???"

Rubi sobbed.

That made his nostrils flare, his temples throb,as disbelief began to weigh Mes'siyah down.

"I'm talking to you, bitch!" he said, seethingly.

Immediately, Rubi began to sob louder as if she was in agonizing pain. Mes' siyah had slapped her in her face a few times for being all up in clubs, allegedly thotting. What would he do to her for fucking with the enemy???

The screen went black. And Mes'siyah stuffed it back in his pocket.

Rubi ran to her room and softly shut the door. She needed to think. There was only one option. Call Angel. She was daddy's little girl, but Mes'siyah was mommy's little boy.

Angel was at a restaurant in Hollywood, eating a Caesar salad all alone. And she didn't mind. She was thinking about the new addition to the family, and how that arrival just might bring everyone back together again.

Rubi's call went to voicemail. Rubi began to pace her room, then she went under the bed and pulled out a gun.

A gun she had stolen from Smally G, in route to New York City.

Angel sat her fork and knife down, and called Rubi back.

"Mom!"

"Hey, you. I was just thinking about you." Rubi said, "Really???"

"I was. And you called me."

"Oh."

Angel said, "A million views on the video. And nearing a half million streams. Kudos to you, and to Avery Trap. I always knew you were special."

"Mom."

"Yes."

"I met a boy."

"You're gonna meet a lot of boys, with that outfit you were wearing in that video, "Angel said, running her hand over her baby bump. "I'm not ready to be a grandma, Rubi King."

"I met him outside Capitol Ridge. You seen me getting out of his Hellcat at the block party last summer. And you got mad at me, accused me of some things. You thought I fucked him in a car on a city block. I swear I didn't. But he had overwhelmed me, and he ate me out, mommy. I had never experienced anything like it."

Trying to not be judgmental, Angel said, "Oh." Then she added, "I'm sorry for overreacting that day, too. And

I should have apologized sooner. But you know me. I'm queen bitch."

"Okay," Rubi said, sitting the gun down. "Listen, mom,

I continued to see him. I brought him to the mansion. I been messing with him for a few months. And today, daddy, showed me a picture of him. Daddy has a picture of him in his phone, mommy. Creeped me out."

"What? You're not talking about Trap God?"

"No. This guy was locked up, and came home in June."

"You sleeping with two guys at the same time?"

"You make me sound like I'm a thot."

To soften the blow, Angel said, "Scandalous, "then giggled a little. "Super scandalous. I hope you're using protection."

Rubi said, "This guy's name is Charlie."

"And how old is this Charlie?" Angel asked her daughter, looking around as if she was being watched.

"Thirty-two."

"Thirty-two?"

"Yes!"

"You sure?"

"I guess..."

"Charlie's mother didn't get killed over the summer, did she, Rubi?"

"She...ah...did."

206

Angel walked to the rest room. There she said, "The guy your dad showed you is Smally G. I dated him when I was seventeen. Charlie and your dad were right hand mans, Rubi. Charlie is forty, not thirty-two. Charlie shot Avery. And, he was trying to shoot me."

"What???"

"I assure you; he knew exactly who you were when he preyed on you. A pretty young woman, vulnerable, naive, eager to step out of the shadows of her family. Now you see why we always wanted to protect you from these vultures!"

"What???"

"He is a dead man walking. I've wanted him dead since he was released from prison."

"He shot Avery Trap?"

"Who...shot...Avery Trap???" Avery Trap asked, having let herself into Rubi's bedroom. "You know who shot me? Who is that on the other end of that line, Rubi?"

"I'm getting on the next flight to Philly."

"Mom, I'm packing. We're about to go to Atlanta. Like, now. So..."

"Is there anything else you need to tell me?"

Rubi had told Angel everything, except the fact that she had tipped off the man her family was hunting for months now.

Angel repeated, "Is there anything else you need to tell me?"

Avery Trap was watching Rubi's red lips like they were the main attraction at a traveling carnival. "Mes'siyah's livid right now, and I don't know what he's gonna do, mom," Rubi said, pushing the pistol under one of the many pillows decorating her bed.

"You guys know who shot me?" Avery Trap quizzed again.

This would not play well, and both Rubi and Angel knew it. Rubi phatically said, "No."

Angel said, "Who is that, Rubi?"

"It's Avery Trap. "

"Give her the phone."

Avery Trap took the phone, said, "You guys know who shot me?"

"If we knew who shot you, we would have saw to it that the person was prosecuted to the fullest. We know people in high places, Avery Trap."

Hearing Angel's voice made Avery Trap think about how she was fucking Angel's husband, and not who had shot her. "Oh. When is the baby due?"

"Sometime in February. Listen child, I have to go. I think it was a great thing that you and Rubi teamed up. Congrats!"

"Okay, thank you, Angel. Goodbye."

Avery Trap handed Rubi back the phone, and went to the window that gave her a view of the pool. Too close for comfort.

Rubi just stared at the phone wondering where Smally G was? Wondering where her brother was?

They were still shooting at each other. And no one was hit. Smally G had evaded persecution.

As they were heading back west, Mes'siyah got a call from Angel. He said, "Yo???"

"Don't be yo'-ing me!"

" MA, I'm a kill ya daughter. I just don't know how yet...

" Sacari shook his head in disgust and disbelief at the words that left Mes'siyah's mouth. Not only was he talking to his mother in pure stupidity, but he was telling her he was going to kill her daughter.

There Sacari was, grieving the loss of his mother, and wondering whether or not his brother would ever see the streets again, and Mes'siyah was putting a bigger part in his family. And Absolutely devoid of any empathy for his friend of thirteen years.

Right there on City Line Avenue, Sacari jumped the fuck out the car while it was still moving at 35 MPH. By the grace of God, Mes'siyah was able to jump the console and grab control of the steering wheel before it collided with another automobile.

There were other homies in the faculty, but not one of them could measure up to Sacari and what he brought to the table.

Once he had control of the vehicle, he grabbed hold

of the phone, "Ma!"

"Yeah. Listen, you better not put your fucking hands on my daughter! Do you hear me???"

"What? I'm ya son. The firstborn. The heir to the throne. And she betrayed this family!"

"Not intentionally. She's not held to the same standard as-"

"That's why I told my dad what the fuck I told him!"

"And what is that?"

"I'm doing my own thing. I'm out!"

Mes'siyah hung up fuming.

And as if Sacari wasn't already pissed the fuck off, Mes'siyah tracked him down traveling the city by foot, talking about,"I'm breaking away from the family. Starting my own thing. You are second in command."

"Nigga! I don't even have a family!" Sacari shouted, then took off. People were out on City Line Avenue and watched as the albino kid, holding two auto weapons in his hands, used his feet to put time and space between him and Mes'siyah.

Sacari had darted through a parking lot that was chained off. He was gone into the darkness. Even with all the power Mes'siyah had, the royalty, dudes weren't lining up to be his comrade. Sacari was the real draw.

"Fuck! Fuck! Fuck!"

Mes'siyah drove through the chains after Sacari,

busting them and ripping the poles holding them right
out the concrete.

BOOG DENIRO

CHAPTER TWENTY-TWO

Bish stalked over to the side door leading to the poolside and back meadow. The sliding door opened with as much as a squeak, just slid to the right and Bish stepped out into the sunlight.

The poolboy was finishing up his duties, emptying it out, while the landscapers attended to the lands. This was to be their last time visiting the compound until next spring. Snow was nearing.

Bish watched the hard workers speak in their native tongue. They were American-Mexican. And, just a working sprightly, wondering where he had gone wrong with his son. Mes'siyah thought labor only meant to give birth, and had never as much as pulled a muscle in his life. With a cup of coffee in one hand and the other gradually grazing his thick beard, Bish just shook his head in disgust and disbelief.

Late last night, on the local news, Bish saw footage of Smally G's Hellcat in a high speed chase. Never before had he wished prison on someone. So, it felt when the chase had been reported as ending without apprehension.The images of the Hellcat riddled, bullet holes everywhere,played repetitiously on the late news, so Bish knew Mes'siyah had tried. But had failed miserably. Thanks to Rubi tipping off her conniving beau.

Having spent two decades in a cage must've given Smally G some super powers. All those years in the weight room had finally paid it forward. Smally G was able to leap from the Hellcat, pull his impaired brother with him, then lower them down into a manhole before pulling the round medal plate back in place, leaving police scratching their heads.

"Mr. King. Your breakfast is ready..."part of the family?

Her moves weren't supposed to feel like she'd overstepped a boundary. She had no motives. Just missed the delivery,

and maybe announced her presence at the wrong time.

"Let me tell you something. My son being intimate with you does not constitute togetherness. So, if you want to continue getting the check cut here, you need to do what I just asked you to do."

The chef headed back inside, knowing that an audience could make people make decisions they would later regret.

Penelope never expected being accepted by Bish and Angel to be a seamless transition. She knew they wanted

214

more for their son. Like, that white girl with the privilege and power and heritage. Ivory Manning. But she didn't anticipate such resistance either.

So, there they stood, Penelope staring at Bish, Bish eyeing her furiously.

Bish said, "I would hate to have to terminate you for abandoning your job, Penelope ..."

"Really?" Penelope sulked, rolling her eyes and neck.

Bish had to admit, she was forming into a diva, and that made the next statement easier, "You're fired. If you need a reference, I'll be happy to supply that. Be gone by the time I'm done eating."

"Reeeeally? For real?" Penelope asked, irate.

"Clearly."

"In that case, I may as well get my last swim in..."

The poolboy had just finished removing the leaves, and was fixing to drain it.

Penelope proceeded to skinny dip. Straight removed her clothes, unabashedly, and dove in like a professional swimmer.

She knew her body was the banana, curves in all the necessary places to drive men wild. So did the poolboy,the gardener too...

It was autumn, but still warm, evidence that global warming was a real thing. Just the day before it was chilly. Now it was almost sixty degrees.

The water felt good to Penelope's soft skin, and she

swam as if she hadn't a worry in the world. It was like the men watching weren't even there. And as she went from the front stroke to the back stroke, she cut her eyes sharply at Bish while swimming by him.

The reality was she knew too much. She'd seen Rubi swimming in vomit.She'd heard detectives grilling Mes'siyah. Mes'siyah had slipped and said some things. She'd seen Avery trap sneaking out of the master bedroom just the day before!!!

Penelope had power.

She would no longer work at the mansion, but she wasn't going away.

Bish was 44-years old, and with those years came a wealth of understanding. Bish knew that she had sunk her claws into Mes'siyah. But he would still go through the move for now. He had to maintain his stronghold, no matter what.

"Watts, I want Penelope removed from the premises. A-sap."

"Penelope???"

"Yeah. Then have her things gathered. I'll make sure she gets them," Bish ordered before finally having his first meal of the day.

Watts was surprised. Not only was she fucking the boss's son, but she was like family. She'd been around nearly as long as he had been.

While Bish ate, watching the news again, Watts

stalled out for as long as he could, secretly hoping Mes'siyah would stroll through the gates and doors in his skinny jeans, dripping in jewels, before this ugliness got irreparable. If not, Bish would come out of this unscathed while Watts would be on Mes'iyah's shit list. None of it was good.

Watts wondered if him telling Bish Penelope no longer wore uniform, and was making her own hours, played any part in her termination?

"...with the new laws in place, even if convicted, Nicolas Heastie cannot automatically be sentenced to life without the possibility of parole. The United States Supreme Court ruled such sentences for minors are unconstitutional..." the news reporter stated outside the police station on 8th and Race. "Child killers don't have to ability to form intent..."

Bish wasn't the only one watching...

In her parent's Delaware County home, Ivory Manning was watching and wondering.

In West Philly, the gang was sitting around, weed smoke everywhere, HD monitor turned all the way up, watching in understandable shock. Nico had just come off the porch...!

From her bedroom, Ivory Manning mouthed, "Poor guy," while wondering if at all, how this would affect Mes'siyah. Being the daughter of a prosecutor, she knew firsthand how friends rolled over on friends.

Cash, looking around at the squad, Mes'siyah and Sacari clearly absent, said, "Young boy turned out to be a cannon... like his brother!"

Lil Mama wasn't tuned in. She was out at the jail, having been dropped off by Mes'siyah.

Bish didn't have one singular thought. To the best of his recollection, he could not recall a time he had come in contact with Nico. But his son had been seen all over the city and all over social media with Nico.

As Bish was finishing up the first meal of his day, Angel had wobbled in looking nice. Rubbing her stomach with one hand, and dropping her Birkin bag on the island top with the other, she said, "Nice haircut..."

Bish just stared.

"It's like you just saw a ghost?" Angel followed up with,

while Bish swallowed the last of his sea-moss smoothie.

"Nice bag," he finally said.

"You purchased it."

"Guess I forgot. I've purchased so many things for you over the years."

"Clearly," Angel said, no smiles though, all business. She sat on a stool at the island, right next to Bish, looked him straight in the eyes.

"What?" he quizzed.

"He got to our daughter." Somberly, Bish replied, "I

know."

"She spoke to you about it?!"

"I spoke with her about it," Bish clarified, animus clearly mounting once again. As if it had ever gone anywhere. Since viewing the surveillance, he had been livid.

"I know you two are extremely close, but I didn't have her down for discussing that kind of stuff with you," Angel returned, he surprises visible.

"We spoke," Bish repeated. But he felt it best he kept what he knew about Rubi's drug abuse to himself for now. It could possibly induce a premature labor, if Angel knew.

Angel said, "Mes'siyah called me last night."

"Okay."

"Threatening to kill Rubi," Angel said, her voice lowering with each word. She didn't want anyone to accidently hear about the family feud. "But I know he isn't working with a full deck. He's crazy."

Bish nodded, sick to his stomach.

"We fucked that boy up," Angel whispered. "That's why I'm here, and not Baldwin Hills. He may need some help, Bishop. Some serious counseling."

"Too late for that, "Bish said, shaking his head. "We're bad parents. Great hustlers! But, very, very bad parents, Angel. And our lives didn't have to be this way. We defied the odds, we leaped over the hurdles, bombarded barriers, got in where they said we didn't fit in. We achieved our goals. But somehow greed is on the cusp of swallowing us whole."

Angel wasn't in total agreement with that assessment, and wore the dissent on her lips as they were poked to the side.

"Where is Rubi now? I was hoping to catch her-"

"Left for Atlanta. Hip Hop Awards. I started pause to put a on it. But she needs to get away from Philly.I think she can be better than both of us, if she gets away..."

At that very moment Rubi was in the back of an all black 2017 Maybach, heading to the airport, with Smally G blowing her phone up. Her luggage was packed, enough clothes for ten awards shows in tow. And she was ready to put the city of Brotherly Love in her rearview for a moment.A brief moment.

There was Smally G! Calling again! He had even tried to cut in via FaceTime.

This time, Rubi answered, and said, "What???" She could see dark and dank concrete walls in the midst of darkness.

"I need you. Can you come scoop me??? Now???"

"No! Hell no, Smally G. That is your name, ain't it? I will not come scoop you."

"Why the fuck not?"

"I'm leaving. Business trip. Bye."

Avery Trap wasn't far away. Just a comfy over on the

other end of the plush and wide back seat, on her phone, and paying Rubi absolutely no mind.

"You talking to me like I'm some poot-put-ass-nigga!"

"Only a poot-put-ass-nigga would take advantage of a young and naive girl, only looking for love and acceptance. You tried to get me hooked on hard drugs, so you could control me. You lied to me about your identity, and you my parents's age. Oh, and you was fucking with my moms back in the days. Kick rocks nigga."

"Rubi...yo...Rubi" he said, his voice echoing loudly in the background.

Rubi caught her client out the corner of her eye. The super talented and wild sexy Avery Trap.

Avery Trap was wearing a white cat suit, black leather red bottom shoes, makeup and hair to die for.

Rubi then went on to say, "Everything that ever came out ya mouth was a lie. Leave Philly. You better be gone by the time I get back. Or face the consequences."

"Fuck you-" Smally G had got out before Rubi had removed his desperate face from her screen.

Having realized the poison, she was smoking wasn't making her sharper, savvier and more lit, but was actually hindering her ability to excel and morph into her higher self, Rubi had the driver pull over on the Ben Franklin Bridge.

"Be right back," Rubi said, exiting the vehicle with

a cheeky smile and her hair blowing in the light winds.

Avery Trap watched as a big fluffy zip lock bag was pulled from Rubi's Birkin bag. She continued to watch intently.

"I'm better than this. I know better. I will do better" Rubi told herself then exhaled as she turned the zip lock upside down and dumped the contents into the river below.

Author's Note....

Thanks for the support! Word up.
The third installment of the URBAN ROYALTY saga
will be released later on this year, entitled:

URBAN ROYALTY 3,
KINGS' LANDING

The drama, the suspense, the thrill will be
supremely heightened!!!!

BOOG DENIRO

ACKNOWLEDGMENTS

Without God laying the path and me taking them steps, none of this would be possible! 2020 was a tough year.

My confidants, whom I cherish, Omar & Naquan, you two believed in me even when I sometime doubted myself. You two understood --geniuses speak their own language -- and, listen whenever I called. I'm quite sure there were better things to do. Well, maybe not during this global pandemic. But, all those other years...certainly. Thank you for believing in me...

Shout out to my nieces and nephews -Zoey, Zuri,Syann,Zahir, Sekani...Special shout out to my siblings - Dell, Sade, Tyasia...

Special thanks to the CHAVEZ-FREED LAW OFFICE. You were studying my case when I didn't even know it. I was in the process of filing for commutation, throwing myself at the mercy of the Pennsylvania Board of Pardons, when you contacted me. That initial call, 95 minutes, I cried when I heard you say, "You're innocent, and I'm sorry you had to go through this. You will be free."And I'm stone to the bone, emotionless. 22-plus years of prison has made me this way. God bless you, your family, and the practice ...

Special shout out to -- John & Michelle Haywood,Floyd Murray, BJ.L(one of a kind), T. Walton, Bay Jarrell, Meek Sanders, DJ Cocoa Chanelle, DJ Wafflas, Nish Way , Casper Hill, Shelly P., Hassan Campbell, Al Duran, my bro Gary Chisholm, Tisha, Latisha, King Turner, Rob Wiesman, Calvin T. Posey, Imani McDonald., my bros Low 456 & Roger Rabb, Tankhead Genile, TaKi a McCreary, DonJaun, Dee Watkins, Angelique, Bugatti Bak, Storm Heastie, Country McRae,Handz Milburne, Dontaye "3" Deshields, Cassarah & Kayla, Mel "Bas" Bethune, my godsons Ball-Out & Tobe Bethune, MamaDon, Razor Reynolds,Jamie-O, Phil Jamison, Gerald Price, G.Garmon (chiraq),Sam Ross,Brandon Key ,Damon Wall, Mac Boney, Montega Thomas, Ronnie Stone,Mike Boogie & Kay-Kay (Macombs Rd), Kay-Kay (the QUIP), Black Star Music & Video, CADBI, Second Chance Ministries (Pastor Boyd), Justice For Youth Foundation (Bro.Khalil Abdul Muhammad), THE FRESH MIX MAGAZINE, WHY MAGAZINE, the bro Cello, and Quan Banks, the blocks that raised me: Tremont & Davidson, 175th & Macombs Road, Bronx New York. Rest in Power - Mommy, Pauline, Larry Mo, Champ, Craig, Sharon Palm, and my dear

226

Jacque line Denise Orr (gone too soon). If I missed anyone, blame my mind, not my heart.
PEACE!!!

S.G. PUBLISHING

URBAN ROYALTY

A BOOG DENIRO PRODUCTION

S.G. PUBLISHING
NEW YORK

CHAPTER TEN

JUNE 29, 2016
SATURDAY 11PM

Outside of Ridge Capitol, Rubi and her girls exited their vehicles and enjoyed the black summer night. It was dark out, but the lights were bright. Street lights, and headlights illuminated the scene.

A white Jaguar honked the horn at them. The 2016 model was breathtaking, big and boss like, looking like luxury. And all four of them took a peek to see who the driver was. The hazard lights come on, and out hopped a muscular fellow, about 180 lbs, his diamonds lighting it up. The swag in his strut, and the pep in his step, exuded confidence. The white *shelltoe* Adidas were new. The white PRP's fit properly. The white and crème Louis Vuitton belt held the gun on his hip close. The fitted white LV Tee allowed his chain to swing, and his Rolex to attract attention. Anyone looking could tell he worked out faithfully, and took good care of his teeth and skin. He was standing about 5'9", and his chocolate skin shone in the night. He walked up to the girls, all his attention on Rubi whom did not look eighteen that night.

Rubi had on a hot pink romper with elastic in the hem

that gripped her calves, showing off her ankles and feet. The fabric was so soft, Rubi's ass just wiggled with each step she took in her high price stilettos. And that day she decided not to wear a bra, so her tits looked lush with the thick nipples penetrating the top part of the romper. She would be nineteen in a few weeks, but appeared to be in her prime.

The chocolate brother licked his lips, took Rubi's hand into his, and said, "What's up, *superstar*?"

Another groupie, she wanted to think, but he resembled a superstar too. And his voice was deep and rugged, and smooth and intoxicating, and made Rubi's girls a bit envious he didn't speak to them. Goose-bumps formed on Rubi's biceps and forearms. *Trap God is cute, but this brother is gorgeous*, she said to herself.

She further observed him from his wavy hair to his sneakers, and said, "Just out, me and *my gurls*."

"And your name is?"

"Rubi…"

"I need your number, Rubi," he said, staring into her eyes. His face was so close to Rubi's, she could smell the Big Red gum on his breath.

She chortled, looking to her girls for approval. While she was doing that, Trap God's small entourage drove by in their small fleet of cars. The guy Mes'siyah had shot in the shoulder was riding shotgun with Trap God, bobbing his head to something by Meek Mill.

Rubi's girl, Imani, was dressed to impressed, had spent her entire allowance to do it too, and made eye contact with one of the main players in the Trap God's outfit. Her parent's held her down, so long as she stayed in college, but she was still in search of a sponsor. Imani's parent's weren't kingpins, they weren't *urban royalty*, they were hardworking middle class folk.

After logging her number in the guy's iPhone, Rubi said, "And who's gonna be calling me?"

"Oh, I'm Charlie."

"And how old are you, Charlie?"

He smiled again, flashing his freshly whitened teeth, and said, "I'll be thirty in a few weeks."

Twenty-nine, thought Rubi, pondering was that too old. *He's got me by ten years.*

"And how *young* are you?" he asked Rubi.

"I be twenty-one,"—she paused—"in a few weeks."

She wasn't a good liar, and dude picked up on that quick. But it didn't matter. Two liars deserved each other.

"What's your sign?" Rubi asked him.

"Cancer," he proudly announced.

"Me too!" Rubi revealed.

She was intrigued on many levels. In some ways he reminded her of Mes'siyah. He didn't have a big fluffy beard, or the tattoos, or the height, but everything else was there. She thought maybe Mes'siyah would iden-tify with dude, and finally accept a man she was show-interest in. She was in a daze, and didn't even feel Charlie's lips on her forehead.

"I gotta go. But I'll be in touch." And with that, Charlie's driver was gone.

The girls went into the club and shut it down for a couple hours. Guys were ogling, gawking, and they loved the attention.

Rubi had an early breakfast with Trap God at a local diner around three that morning, but she was thinking about Charlie's *smooth ass* the whole time. Imani locked in her newest sponsor, as they slid off together.

THE NEXT MORNING, Rubi showered, slipped into some shorts and a cute Tee, so she could just lounge around the mansion in comfort. Maybe Charlie would call??? Maybe he was at church??? Maybe they could spend their birthdays together???

It was around 10:00 AM when Rubi smelled the aroma of French toast. She headed towards the wonderful scent, singing a tune by Trey Songz.

Meanwhile, on the other side of the residence, Mes'siyah was just rising from slumber too. He had partied hard the night before too, out in New York with Mally Gz and his Bronx crew.

"Good morning, Mes'siyah," a high yellow house-keeper said, as she dusted a vase by the TV room.

"Morning to you too, Bev," Mes'siyah shot back.

"Will you be having breakfast with the family?"

"No. Won't even be here that long."

"Okay," Beverly said, as Mes'siyah made his way to the vault. He had picked up a grip of cash from Mally Gz while in New York, most of which belonged to his parents. After putting his cut up, he headed to Bish's office, taking the secret door, which he just found out his mother had been traveling through too lately. The other night he heard them in there *fucking*.

His phone rang. It was Sacari.

"Yo, Bro," Mes'siyah said, entering the secret door.

"I'm ready," Sacari replied.

"Alright, I'm on my way."

Mes'siyah was about to hang up, when Sacari said, "Tell Rubi to keep her lil ass out Capitol Ridge. All the dope boys was all over her lil crew, Bro."

"Clearly." Mes'siyah put the cash where it belonged, then unzipped the duffels. "Thanks, Bro."

"See you when you get here."

"Clearly." Mes'siyah hung up. He had corrupted Sacari's little brother, but he wanted to keep his little sister *pure*.

Two at a time, Mes'siyah tossed kilos into three duffels, then stuffed the bags into the trunk of the Bentley. Once done, he snickered, walking back into the mansion, and towards his family whom were congregating though in their own worlds.

Uneasy, Bish was reading the newspaper while picking at his food. Angel was checking out an article in Essence magazine about breast feeding, while sipping a cold glass of orange juice. Fucking up some scrambled eggs and French toast, Rubi was doing some online shopping.

"Old head..."

"Young boy..."

"Momma..."

"My Mes'siyah..." Angel replied, smiling at him.

Rubi looked up, wondering why she wasn't greeted, only to see a right hand coming at her.

Swattt!

The sound made the smack seem much worse than it really was. Rubi had dipped that shit and slid down off the high sitting stool, falling on her ass.

Bish quickly rose from his thoughts in disbelief, asking, "Yo, young boy, fuck is you doing?"

Angel grabbed Bish's hand, and shook her head *no*. She tapped his hand, and he sat back down as if he were trained.

Mes'siyah leaned down and swung an open hand at Rubi's pretty face again, connecting a bit more flush that time. And it dazed Rubi. She was seeing stars.

He grabbed her by her long lustrous hair, pulling her to the center of the ground floor. "You think it's a game? Shit ain't a game, lil girl!"

Rubi screamed, "Daddy!"

Bish couldn't watch. He felt weak, docile, unmanly, and helpless, and couldn't believe Angel was actually holding him back.

Once Mes'siyah got Rubi where he wanted her, he began to site her disrespect. "I told you to stay out the city, you still go there. I tell you to stay out the clubs, you all up in the clubs. I tell you to keep them niggas out ya face, they all up in ya grill. You just don't get it. Until ya ass get kidnapped, and they send a ransom note. Or, you get touched for some foul shit ya family did."

Angel whispered to Bish, "That's why you let it play out, daddy."

Mes'siyah continued, "And when those things happen, Daddy gonna blame me. Mommy gonna want me to get out there in those streets and bring ya ass back to the King compound."

Rubi wept senselessly, and until Mes'siyah released her from his grasp. She got up and rolled her eyes at Angel. She turned her nose up at Bish. The maids and the cooks got back to work, fearing Rubi's wrath.

Bish felt like shit, while Angel moved on to an article in the Philadelphia Daily News about a new DA looking to come in and clean the office up.

When Angel felt Bish peering down on her with strained eyes, she looked up and said, "She's been lying to us the entire time about where she's been going when she leaves here. And she's too big for us to be beating her."

"Beating her?" Bish snapped. "The damn girl will be nineteen in a few weeks. She's *grown!*"

"Still need checks and balances in her life," Angel countered. "And she's under our roof."

"Angel, do me a favor," Bish asked.

"Anything for you, my king," Angel said, sitting the newspaper down on the island top, giving Bish here undivided attention.

Without reservation, Bish said, "Shut the fuck up!"

Before Angel could say or do anything in response, Bish went on saying, "You posting all our business on social media is how the fuck Smally knew we were in New York. We all gots to tighten the fuck up!" And with that, he left her sitting alone, almost brushing shoulder's with Mes'siyah who was in shock that his father had spoken to his mother in that fashion.

Angel dropped her head, shut her eyes, and prayed. She prayed for her family's safety and protection, for a healthy full term pregnancy, and that this trying time wouldn't put a strain on her marriage.

Deep down, she knew things were about to take a turn for the worse.

Silent, and slowly, Mes'siyah stalked out...shaking his head. In his mind, this was all Rubi's fault. Not the lifestyle their parents perpetuated, and brought them up in.

BOOG DENIRO

The book that started it all!!!!

FIVE STAR REVIEWS
★★★★★
AVAILABLE ON **AMAZON**

Respect The Struggle

By BOOG DENIRO

Read an excerpt...

S.G. PUBLISHING

CHAPTER 1

Split Decisions

"Ta-Ta! Ta-Ta, come here!" I heard my younger sister Shavon cry. "Hurry up pleeeease!"

I was in my mother's room watching cartoons when the hollering of my litter brother also fell on my ears. "What happened?" I asked, gaiting through the living room towards the kitchen. There I saw tears streaming Shavon's pretty face. And melted flesh failing from Rashid's bare chest as he lay on the filthy kitchen floor in severe pain, only a foot from a puddle of scolding hot water and steaming pot.

"Damn, what happened?" I asked, worried sick.

"He grabbed the pot handle and the hot water fell on him."

"What the fuck was you doing?"

"Making some Oodles-of-noodles," she cried. "I was hungry. Please don't tell on me?" she begged.

BOOG DENIRO

"You just came home from school, how was you hungry?!" I responded, scooping Rashid up in my arms.

"Hurt," he wailed, breathing heavily.

"Don't touch it, baby boy," I told him, rushing him to my mother's room, with no idea how long it would be before she'd return. Every day the wind blew her in at different times. I laid him across the bed then paced the tiny room.

We didn't have a phone, and we weren't allowed to leave the apartment, so there was nothing I could do. And even if there was, authorities would want to know what an eleven year old, a nine year old, and a two year old were doing home unsupervised.

With my moms being strung out on crack, things were already fucked up. But, Sabrina not coming home until 9:30 that night took things to a deeper and darker state. Her negligence, along with the unfortunate accident, would launch a full fledge investigation by the Bureau of Child Welfare, which would expose not only her insatiable crack addiction, but a long tale of child abuse.

The minute Sabrina stuck her key into the front door, Shavon took flight, seeking refuge beneath her bed. Having witnessed her beat me with anything she could get her hands on—*broom stick, skillets, extension cord*—Shavon wanted no parts.

"Where y'all at?" Sabrina quizzed upon her entry. "I know y'all hungry."

You damn right!, I thought, knowing she knew there was nothing to eat in the crib when she left that morning

S.G. PUBLISHING

in chase of the almighty dollar. But I would never say that, knowing she'd knock the shit out of me.

However, I managed to get out, "Sabrina, ya son got burnt!"

She replied, "What? How the fuck that happened? Yo ass was *suppose* to be watching him! I'ma fuck you up!"

I *was* watching him, just as I was accustom to her fuckin' me up. I'd missed damn near two months of school watching Rashid every day, while she ran the streets.

Sabrina raced over to her bedside and examined the wound. "Goddammit!" she exclaimed, having yet to remove her leather coat and scarf. He was lying there drinking a bottle filled with sugar and water.

"Ta-Ta, I'ma really fuck you up, now!!"

Use to the abuse, I didn't even react. I was just glad my boy would finally be getting some medical attention. I could take her blows to the face. What I couldn't take was not being able to hear Rashid laugh.

BOOG DENIRO
C.E.O. /FOUNDER
S.G. PUBLISHING